*"Sam, I don't like the idea
of your being down there alone.
It'll be dark soon, and I'm sure
Brad's capable of anything—"*

She placed a fingertip to his lips. "I'm the detective. Remember? I can handle myself." Her blue eyes traveled over Joel's face. "Darling, another thing. If we should—" She paused. "If we should be separated somehow, I'll meet you at the Monroe mansion tomorrow evening."

He seized her shoulders. "Sam, I have no intention of being separated from you. That's crazy, not to mention dangerous!" He cupped his palms on either side of her face. "Don't take any unnecessary chances, Sam. Promise?"

"I'll do my best," she breathed, her voice a whisper in the twilight...

Hilary Cole *has enjoyed writing since she was old enough to put a pen to paper. She lives with her husband and two sons in Kansas, where she helps run the family furniture business. An avid golfer and enthusiastic spectator of her sons' sporting competitions, she also loves movies—especially romantic comedies of the 1930s and '40s.*

Dear Reader:

One of the most exciting things about creating TO HAVE AND TO HOLD has been watching it emerge from the glimmer of an idea, into a firm concept, and finally into a line of books that is attracting an ever-increasing and loyal readership. TO HAVE AND TO HOLD is now eleven months old, and that thrilling growth continues every month as we work with more and more talented writers, find brand new story ideas, and receive your thoughts and comments on the books.

More than ever, we are publishing books that offer all the elements you love in a romance—as well as the freshness and variety you crave. When you finish a TO HAVE AND TO HOLD book, we trust you'll experience the special glow of satisfaction that comes from reading a really good romance with a brand new twist.

And if any of your friends still question whether married love can be as compelling, heart-warming, and just plain fun as courtship, we hope you'll share your latest TO HAVE AND TO HOLD romance with them and dispel their doubts once and for all!

Best wishes for a fabulous summer,

Ellen Edwards

Ellen Edwards, Senior Editor
TO HAVE AND TO HOLD
The Berkley Publishing Group
200 Madison Avenue
New York, N.Y. 10016

P.S.   Do you receive our SECOND CHANCE AT LOVE and TO HAVE AND TO HOLD newsletter? If not, be sure to fill out the coupon in the back of this book, and we'll send you the newsletter free of charge four times a year.

MY DARLING DETECTIVE

HILARY COLE

SECOND CHANCE AT LOVE
BOOK

To Janice and Andrea—without whom
I would never have begun.
And to my friends and family—
without whom I would
never have finished.

With special appreciation
to Dede,
who knew what
I wanted to do
before I did.

MY DARLING DETECTIVE

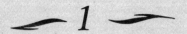

1

Samantha Lacey Loring sighed audibly and shoved the pile of papers on her desk to one side. She was restless—and a little worried. Ever since she'd taken over her father's private investigating business, things had seemed to go steadily downhill. Admitting the reason for her distress caused the smooth brow under the tumbled blond curls to wrinkle in thought. And then the objectivity that was such a necessary part of her trade slowly surfaced, making her realize business hadn't really been so good even in the last year of her father's life.

She reflected on this for a moment and then dug deep into a drawer of the old-fashioned, oak roll-top desk. Seconds later, she found what she was looking for and, with perverse delight, crammed the Sherlock Holmes–style hat on her head. It had been a gag gift for her last birthday. Rummaging in the pencil tray, she closed her fingers over her father's pipe. She stuck it in the corner of her mouth and walked over to the mirror above the chipped sink.

Ah, perfect, she thought. Tilting her head in defiance at her own reflection, Samantha reconsidered. Well, maybe not *perfect*, but at least good for a giggle or two. This outfit made her look more the part anyway. Adjusting the brim of the hat, she eyed herself critically. She had to admit she wasn't quite the image of the master detective, but the costume did lend an air of authority to her decidedly feminine appearance.

Leaning closer to the mirror, Samantha launched into a spirited dialogue: "Now, Watson, if the butler didn't stuff that body into the dumbwaiter, then who did? Perhaps it was Mrs. Rotworth—she, of all the guests, had the ideal motive, the—"

"But I ask you, members of the jury, did she have the *opportunity?*" a familiarly resonant voice proclaimed behind her.

Samantha wheeled around, her cheeks flushing to a deep apricot. "Joel! What are you doing here, darling? It's not even five o'clock yet."

Joel Loring casually leaned his rangy frame against the doorjamb, his dark eyes flashing mischievously. The collar of his khaki trench coat was turned up, accenting his square, clefted chin and his bronzed coloring. "Sam, you do have a way with words. No wonder I was the only man who had the nerve to ask for your hand in marriage."

Samantha shook her head adamantly, threatening to dislodge her perilously arranged topknot. *"Au contraire.* Every man likes a woman who plays the aloof, unattainable female. After all, why do you think Garbo kindled the desire of men the world over? Why do you—"

Joel crossed the room in three long-legged strides, and Samantha's dramatic pronouncements faded against the warmly insistent pressure of her husband's mouth.

"Hmmm... You taste delicious," he murmured.

"So do you." She drew back slightly to trace the lean, hard lines of his face, letting her finger come finally to rest in the dimpled cleft of his chin. "Mister, after six months of marriage, you're still my all-time favorite kisser."

Joel chuckled and slid his hand to cup one of Samantha's silken-clad buttocks. "Yeah? Well, I hope you won't ever demote me from that category because my kissing is just a preliminary—an appetizer, as it were." The pressure of his fingers increased on her hip and moved slowly down her slender thigh.

"Speaking of appetizers," Samantha whispered against his throat, "are you early because you're hungry?"

"Hmmm...Starving!" Joel's lips nibbled at the delicate shell of her ear. "I'm absolutely ravenous!"

Samantha moaned slightly as his thighs pressed into hers, their taut, muscular thrust conveying the urgency of Joel's message. "So, you're in the mood for love—not spaghetti—is that it?" she asked breathlessly.

"Ah, you're good—very good," Joel answered huskily, both hands now clasping her well-shaped derrière so that her body melded perfectly with his. "Of course, I should expect such spectacular deductions from a private detective."

Samantha shifted uneasily in her husband's embrace and shot him a lopsided smile. "Well, it's a relief to know my husband respects my professional ability at least. One tends to lose the old know-how when one doesn't have any real cases to keep the mind sharp." She'd intended the words to have a lofty ring, but somehow they sounded more like a complaint.

"What's this? Feeling sorry for yourself? My Samantha? Famous lady gumshoe?" Joel drew her into the circle of his arm and gently thrust her chin up with his thumb. Seeing the apprehension in those enormous turquoise eyes caused him to drop his attempt at lighthearted banter. "Sam?"

Samantha pushed at the combs in her tumbled curls, trying to tuck in the forever-straying tendrils. The fringe of her long, dark lashes lowered to conceal the disappointment and frustration in her astonishingly blue eyes as she bit her lip. But the increasing pressure of Joel's thumb under her chin finally forced her to look back into his face.

"I—I, Joel, I so much wanted to restore this detective agency to what it once was—and I'm not getting anywhere. Even though I'm darned good at my job! All I've had lately are a few little cases here and there—finding missing pets, spying on errant spouses, catching fake whiplash victims water skiing...Nothing I can really sink my teeth into."

Joel lovingly brushed a shiny strand of recalcitrant hair from her face. "Darling, you can't expect miracles overnight. It takes a long time to establish a business—and you know your dad deliberately slowed things down when his heart started going bad. He didn't want to take on strenuous, exhausting cases. He left those for Perry Mason..." Joel rubbed his knuckles along Samantha's cheek. "It just takes time," he repeated softly.

She managed a weak smile and turned toward the window. The blue-gray haze of the horizon was misting into dusk and the street lights had come on. Rush-hour traffic was beginning, the incessant beeping of horns audible even through the closed window of the third-story office.

How many times had she stood here with her father, watching this same scene? He'd been gone nearly four months. It was hard to imagine how the big, raw-boned man with the roughly hewn features of a Viking warrior could succumb to, as he put it, "a bad ticker." Oh, how she missed him! He'd been the only parent she'd ever really known.

Her mother had died when she was a toddler, leaving her father and her to their own devices in the old-fashioned apartment above the agency. But there had been lots of good times—meals at Tony's, movies at the old theater a block farther away, animated discussions of her father's latest case...

"Sam, love, let's wander down the street to Tony's and have a nice glass of wine—maybe even a little pasta. Then we'll head for home and relax. What do you say?" Joel's hands closed around her cashmere-sweatered shoulders as he pulled her against the crispness of his trench coat.

Samantha felt a surge of love for him. Joel knew her so well. He understood she needed to leave the office so she could talk freely, unhindered by memories of her father, her early years, all of the dreams she'd so carefully nourished for the future: she and her father working together, solving interesting cases, going upstairs to the apartment for coffee...

She spun around, determined to free herself of the blues, and clasped Joel around the neck. "I say you're absolutely right, husband of mine. In fact, let's leave the car here and walk to Tony's—draw some of this frosty autumn air into our lungs!"

"You're on, kid!" Joel placed a hand on either side of her face, massaging her temples with his thumbs. Lecherously, he added, "I know how sexy you can be after a dinner of pasta. So let's not waste anymore valuable time!"

Samantha smiled. This *is* what I need, she thought: a contented tummy and my husband to make love to me. The prospect of both suddenly seemed the best answer in the world to her troubles. She kissed Joel fervently, running her hands through the dark hair that curled above his collar.

The enthusiasm of the kiss escalated into more than either of them had expected. Joel's tongue eased its velvety way into Samantha's mouth, shooting small, fiery darts of pleasure as it crept among the secret, sensitive tissues. A muffled moan escaped her lips as Samantha arched her lean body against Joel's thighs. The responding hardness aroused her even more and her hand slid from the back of his neck down to stroke the burgeoning evidence of his desire.

"Oh, Joel, I love you so much," she murmured into his ear.

"And I love you, Sam. You're my most favored, most desired lady detective..." His voice trailed off as he reclaimed her full mouth.

At that moment the door opened, and a small, gray-haired woman staggered in carrying a large, gold Persian cat under one arm. "He was hanging around at the restaurant down the street again. As if he doesn't get fed well enough right here!"

Samantha and Joel broke apart hurriedly and turned

to face the scowling woman. "Uh, thanks for finding him, Miss Davenport. We were just—"

"Leaving," Joel supplied quickly. "We're both starving," he added lamely.

"It's fine if you two want to go," Miss Davenport barked in a voice twice as big as she was. "I've got nothing to do lately but knit, anyway." Casting a haughty, sidelong look at Joel and Samantha, she dropped the enormous cat to let him wander about the office.

Samantha chuckled. Her father's long-time secretary had walked in on a scene that undoubtedly struck her as a few notches down the X-rated scale from Doris Day! Bending over to disguise her amusement, Samantha scooped her arrogant pet up into her arms.

"How are you, Dr. Watson? How's my big boy?" she cooed into the cat's neck, hoping her smile was safely hidden in his fur.

Self-consciously, Joel reached over to scratch Watson's ears and received a swat by a not-so-dainty paw.

"Watson! Shame on you!" Samantha scolded. "Joel's part of the family. When are you going to accept that?"

Joel shrugged eloquently. "Let's face it, Sam. Watson and I are never going to be the best of friends. As far as he's concerned, I'm still an interloper. And it still hurts," he added somberly.

"Bosh!" Miss Davenport shouted. "Watson just knows who belongs in this agency and who doesn't. If you don't mind my saying so, Joel, you ought to stick to your video games firm. Samantha doesn't need any distractions. No, sir! She needs to keep her mind on business during working hours." The old secretary gave her rimmed spectacles a vicious poke. "Why, I remember in the fifties, this place was booming. When your father was alive—and feeling well, Samantha—pooh, this place was busy all the time."

Samantha's shoulders slumped slightly. "I *know*, Miss Davenport. Not only do I remember, but you've reminded me before—many, many times," she said somewhat dejectedly. "Besides, I was Dad's full-fledged partner during some of his biggest cases of recent years," she added proudly. "So I know a boom from a depression!" Drawing herself up to her full five feet nine inches, she glared at the secretary in what she hoped was a stern way. "And, Miss Davenport, I do want to make it clear that I don't view Joel as a distraction."

"Humph! I can't help it if I call 'em as I see 'em," the old lady retorted. Adjusting her glasses so they slid to the end of her rather pointed nose, Miss Davenport plopped into a chair and began typing with a vengeance.

Samantha stole a glance at Joel, and was relieved to see that his face showed none of the signs of impending anger. "Darling, why don't we get going? I really have worked up an appetite."

"Me, too. Rejection always makes me hungry," he said good-humoredly, in the direction of Miss Davenport's rigid back.

Samantha leaned over and kissed his cheek. "Thanks," she whispered. Her voice was almost drowned out by the clacking typewriter keys. "She really doesn't dislike you, you know. She just never could stand having a man in this office except my father—unless, of course, he happens to be a client."

"I know," Joel whispered back. "Why do you think I usually wait outside for you? It's safer if I don't cross paths with Watson and Miss Davenport very often!"

Samantha gave Joel a playful punch and, grabbing her coat from the hall tree, blew kisses to Watson, who had curled up lazily on her desk. "See you tomorrow, mouse-catcher!"

Once outside in the dimly lit hall of the large, six-story office building, Samantha let out a groan that was halfway between laughter and exasperation. "I'm sorry, darling. I'm afraid both my cat and my secretary are really just plain possessive."

Joel slid his arm around her shoulders as they walked the length of the hallway, which was dotted with the doors of different firms. "I can understand perfectly well why they'd be possessive of you, Sam. I feel the same way. May be that's because we moved around so much when I was a kid—made it kind of hard to establish lasting relationships."

Joel hoped his comments had come off in a cavalier fashion. His last intention was to smother Samantha with possessiveness. Yet it was true he placed a high premium on mutually binding ties between people. His trust was not easily won, but once given, his expectations were high.

As the only child of an Army colonel, he'd had the military philosophy of loyalty ingrained in him since he was old enough to understand the concept. Never take anything or anyone at face value, he believed. But once a person's trustworthiness has been established, prize that quality above all else. And, most of all, reciprocate it.

Samantha, with her independent courage and the whimsical, bubbling charm he adored, was everything in the world to him. He remembered how impressed he'd been with her sense of honor, her abiding loyalty to her father. That she had fallen in love with Joel was one of the miracles of his life. He was grateful for the sharing camaraderie of their marriage, the unspoken trust that made it possible to discuss everything together.

He frowned guiltily, pulling Samantha a little closer. Fervently, he wished he could tell her what was bothering him right now. But it wasn't fair to burden her with what might turn out to be nothing—especially since she was still trying to recover from the shock of her father's death. He had been her whole family for so long...

No, he couldn't cause more problems for Samantha now. This was *his* problem, and he wouldn't burden her with it. She didn't need to deal with any unsettling emotions until she had her life totally back together again. Joel only hoped he was a good enough actor to convince her nothing was wrong.

As they walked past the constantly non-functioning elevator to the stairs, Samantha bumped her lean hip into Joel's, suggestively. The electric response the movement elicited was apparent, even through the protection of her coat. On the next step, Joel bumped her back. They continued the game down three flights of stairs.

"Keep that up and you'll never make it to dinner," Joel warned, opening the door that led to the first floor.

"I have nothing to fear," she teased. "Look at that crowd in the lobby waiting for their car-pool rides. How would they react if you were to throw me to the floor right now? Hmmm?"

"Enviously!"

Laughing happily, arm in arm, Joel and Samantha exchanged "good nights" with various familiar faces among the cluster of people in the foyer and pushed open the heavy glass doors. A frosty onslaught of cold air greeted them and they turned up their coat collars to walk the brisk block to the neighborhood restaurant, Tony's Italian Gardens.

Samantha slid her arm through Joel's, not unaware of the admiring glances they drew as they strode through the city streets. This part of the metropolis of Milburne, Kansas, was very old, once the heart of the business district. However, in the last twenty years, outlying suburban areas and newer developments thirty blocks east had, with their gleaming chrome and steel structures, caused this region to remain essentially the same—suspended in time.

Samantha recognized every faded landmark, many of the pedestrians' faces, and all of the cab drivers. This was where she'd grown up, in an apartment above the agency, in this relatively unchanging neighborhood. Her childhood friends had been shopkeepers, bartenders, secretaries, tailors, and the managers of movie theaters. While the sameness of her formative years had influenced her experiences and philosophies, the diversity of Joel's had contributed to his. He'd moved around so much as a child that the few permanent attachments he managed to make and keep were paramount in his life.

I'm glad I'm one of them, Samantha thought, glancing at her handsome husband, who gave her his I-love-you smile and then linked her arm more firmly through his.

"Feeling better?" Joel asked.

"I always feel better when I'm with you," she answered truthfully. "Besides, it's great to see a new face in this old neighborhood!"

"Uh-huh," Joel agreed. "Without me to add sparkle to your life, you've got to admit your memoirs could be pretty boring!"

Tony's was crowded. Samantha spotted the pudgy owner carrying a huge tray of steaming food to a table and waved. "Hello, Samantha! Hey, Joel! Sick of your own cooking again? Have a seat. Rosie or I will be right with you."

Samantha and Joel nodded, making their way to the rear of the restaurant. A table for two near a window was unoccupied. Just as they were sinking into their chairs, a familiar voice called to them over the din of the crowd.

"It's Brad!" Joel cried, enthusiastically motioning to his friend and employee to join them.

Samantha's heart gave a little lurch. She'd really wanted to spend the evening alone with her husband. Two or three nights a week she and Joel found themselves at Tony's among familiar faces, but usually none familiar enough to invade the privacy they treasured.

As the tall, handsome blond man approached their table, Joel stood to greet his friend. "Brad, what a surprise! Here, have a seat."

"Hi, Brad," Samantha said pleasantly. "Please. Sit down."

Brad shot them a neon smile, straddling the extra chair

between Joel and Samantha. "I heard you two often stopped here after work. And I was in the neighborhood—so I thought I'd see if Tony's food is really as terrific as you claim."

"Good food—and now, good company," Joel responded heartily.

"You're sure I'm not intruding?"

"Absolutely not."

"Of course not," Samantha agreed. "We're always glad to see you," she added, *though not tonight,* she thought. The moment the thought crossed her mind, she felt guilty. After all, it wasn't Brad's fault she was upset over the agency's lack of business. And it wasn't his fault she was really missing her father right now. Brad had no way of knowing that what she needed most tonight was Joel's singular comfort. And Brad was a friend— her husband's best male friend, in fact. She could always seek Joel's solace later.

Fixing a maternal look on Brad, she said sternly, "Where've you been keeping yourself, fellow? I haven't seen you in several days, and we're used to having you around at least once a week!"

Brad folded his arms across his chest, one eyebrow raised in mock disapproval. "Samantha! You don't really want to hear the X-rated details of my social life, do you? I realize you're a sophisticated married lady, but still!"

Joel and Samantha exchanged amused looks. Brad's exploits with women were well known. Tall, slim, and blond, Brad Davies exuded an effervescent charm that impressed business associates and knocked most women off their feet. In fact, Samantha had rarely seen him with the same woman twice.

"I don't know how you manage to have the energy to be so good at your job," Samantha remonstrated playfully. "But Joel insists you're a top P.R. man."

Brad grinned. "Oh, I'm into relations, that's for sure!

Redheads, brunettes, blondes..."

Joel groaned. "I keep forgetting what an awful sense of humor you have!"

Brad grinned in delight, then broke into a hearty chuckle that attracted the attention of several nearby patrons. "Sorry, pal. I just can't resist making you groan."

Joel shook his head. "Sometimes I wonder why I invited you to leave that ad agency in Minneapolis. It's been a rough four months with you as second in command at Hyperspace. Hell! Come to think of it, I don't know why I hired you. You don't even have a computer science background!"

"But you have—" Samantha began.

"A way about you," Joel finished.

"Exactly," Samantha replied, her blue eyes dancing with merriment. "And a certain kind of—"

"Dubious charm," Joel supplied.

"Exactly," Samantha agreed.

It was Brad's turn to groan. "You two! You're incredible—finishing each other's sentences, anticipating one another's thoughts..." His light blue eyes turned serious for a moment. "If I didn't have you as a model, I don't know if I'd believe in marriage."

"What makes you think we don't go home and knock each other's teeth out?" Samantha challenged mischievously.

Brad's expression regained its exuberance. "Not a chance. Your feelings are written all over both your faces. True love is what I see and true love is what you've got! You're very lucky people."

"What a nice thing to say," Samantha commented, genuinely touched. She covered Joel's hand with her own, delighting in the responding pressure of his fingers. Brad was right. She was fortunate to have found a partner as skillfully attuned to her emotional needs as to the physical craving of her body. "It's nice to know my husband's oldest friend approves of his choice," she added.

"Absolutely!" Brad boomed. "And I'll tell you this, Samantha. Even if Joel and I do go way back, if I'd seen you first—"

"Hey! Wait a minute!" Joel cried, shaking a finger playfully in Brad's face. "Nice talk, pal! Always want what I have, don't you?" He grimaced. "I remember Laurie Ann, the cheerleader. I got one date with her and you asked her out the next week—and then the week after that . . . Some friend you were!"

Brad lit a cigarette, obviously enjoying their comfortable repartee. "Yeah? Well, it's not my fault the Army stationed your father in Minneapolis the whole time we were in junior high, and that we ended up in competition for a lot of the same things. Hell's bells, Joel," he added, grinning lazily, "I'm probably the only guy who could ever give you a real run for your money!"

"Is that so? Well, let me just set you straight on a thing or two."

As the two men began to reminisce about their days together in Minneapolis, Samantha watched them fondly. Having a best friend was special, she had to admit. It was a privilege she'd never been granted, or at least allowed herself. Her close association with her father had filled her life, along with only the most casual of chums, certainly none of whom even came close to equalling the place Brad held in Joel's affections.

Tony came to take their orders, interrupting the good-natured exchange between the two men. After introductions were completed between Brad and Tony and menu selections made, the conversation shifted to Hyperspace and Joel's newly invented game, Catwalk.

"I'm telling you, Joel, I really think you're onto something big this time," Brad said admiringly. He turned to Samantha. "Has he told you all about our latest video property?"

She nodded, sipping delicately at the wine Rosie had placed in front of them. "Yes. I think it's terribly exciting. I wish I understood the computer business better; I always feel like I ask the dumbest questions." She sighed. "But Catwalk seemed fairly straightforward. I could certainly understand Joel's enthusiasm."

Joel drifted his fingers lovingly along her smooth cheek. "Honey, I don't understand your business either, but I can still appreciate what it means to you. So we're even."

Brad leaned forward, twirling the stem of his wineglass between his fingers. "How is the detective game, Samantha?"

She forced herself to smile. "Oh, not as profitable or as busy as Hyperspace, I'm afraid. Maybe people are reluctant to hire a woman private investigator—one without a male partner, that is. Or maybe Dad just slowed down so much at the end that other agencies have filled the gap. I'd love to restore the agency to full-line investigation again—the way it was when Dad first made me his partner." As she finished speaking, she realized her tone had been more wistful than she'd intended.

"So you're not interested in staying home and making babies, huh?" Brad asked lightly. "You'd make a terrific mother, Samantha."

She reminded herself that Brad, as a P.R. man, was used to defusing potentially explosive topics of conversation. "Not now. We have plenty of time for that. Joel and I agree on this," she added firmly.

Before either man could respond, Tony appeared at the table with their food. "Here you go, folks! Best pasta in town! Enjoy yourselves and let me know if you need anything else."

"I think we've got everything we need, Tony," Joel said happily, his sculpted cheekbones glowing from both the wine's effect and his enthusiasm. Raising his glass, he made a toast. "To my wife and my best buddy. Here's to many more happy times together."

2

OUTSIDE TONY'S, SAMANTHA AND JOEL waved good-bye to Brad. Then, bracing themselves against the bitingly cold wind, they walked back to the parking area behind the building in which the agency was housed. Samantha eased her long legs into Joel's sleek, foreign sports car, making a face. "Oh, boy, this vehicle's bad for digestion! My stomach jams against my rib cage everytime I sit in these low-slung seats."

Joel gave her an exaggerated wink as he fired the powerful engine into action and swung skillfully into the traffic. "Honey, love me, love my car."

Samantha laid her hand on Joel's thigh. "You can *never* doubt my love, Joel. Any woman who's as tall as I am and who is willing to scrunch up like a jack-in-the-box just to allow her husband to keep his toy, has got to be crazy about him!"

"Is that so? Well, for your information, Mrs. Loring, you were the first lady who ever complained about this car. Most women were really impressed."

Samantha moved her hand higher on Joel's leg. "They must have been midgets," she retorted, increasing the rotating motion of her fingers.

"Hmmm . . . That feels good. Don't stop."

Samantha moved closer, allowing her long fingers to inch slowly up his inner thigh. But in spite of her playfulness, she felt her mood shifting back to her earlier frustration. "Is it too much to want it all—fun, laughter, and mutual success?"

15

Joel's thick, dark brows shot up at her serious undertone.

"Sam, we *do* have it all. I think you're just a little despondent because of your dad's death. I know business at the agency isn't so hot right now, but it'll pick up, honey. Take one day at a time."

Samantha's mouth compressed into a thin line. Joel, who usually was so understanding, seemed to be dishing out nickel psychology and platitudes instead of support. "Well, I guess that's easy for you to say. After all, Hyperspace is going great guns. You've invented a new game you tell me will be really hot as soon as you work out a few bugaboos. So what's to worry?" she added, immediately regretting her rare bout of testiness.

Joel's handsome features tensed in the dim light of the dashboard, but he spoke evenly. "Sam, you've had your private investigator's license since you were twenty-two and before your dad became so ill, you were his right-hand-man. There's no reason to believe you won't be successful on your own. Be patient."

"I'm trying, Joel."

He reached out and caught her hand firmly in his, continuing to steer the little car adeptly through the city streets. "I want you to be completely happy, Sam—and if that means chasing some spy into another galaxy— well, so be it." He looked at her quickly and then directed his attention back to the traffic.

She knew he hoped he'd placated her with his touch of humor, but it was indignation and frustration she felt, not amusement. Turquoise eyes flashed in the dark interior of the car. "I just hope you understand how much my succeeding in my job means to me, Joel. Ever since we've been married, all my job's been is sort of a pleasant little hobby. But I want to turn this avocation into a vocation! I want to restore the agency to full-line investigation again!"

"Sam, I don't want to argue, okay? Let's take everything a step at a time. For now, can't you believe I want what's best for you?"

For a split second, Samantha considered challenging him, but as she turned to answer she noticed how tired he looked. There were faint, dark smudges beneath the thickly lashed eyes and the crinkle lines around his mouth seemed deeper than usual. Guilt overtook her. Something was wrong. Why had Joel come into the office so early today? Suddenly his explanation of being starved for her company didn't ring completely true.

"Joel, what's the matter? Is there something you're not telling me?" she asked anxiously.

He sighed audibly. "Sam, you know we don't keep things worth talking over from each other... I'm just tired. There seems to be a little problem at the office. But I think there's probably a logical explanation for it. The computer's fouled up again. I just need to figure out what I've done wrong."

For the first time in their relationship, Samantha had the strangest feeling Joel wasn't being completely honest with her. Her stomach gave a little lurch. Had she been so totally preoccupied with her own troubles that she'd failed to be the good listener she usually was? Or was she guilty of not reading between the lines? Maybe Joel was trying to protect her from something.

She tried again, laying her hand back on his leg. "Darling, are you sure nothing's really wrong? I mean, maybe we can talk about it and figure the problem out together."

"Sam, it's just a computer foul-up. No real problem, so far as I know." Joel averted his eyes from the road for an instant, giving her his most dazzling smile, the same one he'd turned on her the first time they met in a crowded department store.

The standard joke between them was they'd met in lingerie, but actually it had been on the way to the elevator, which just happened to have been placed next to the nightgowns, panties, and bras. Samantha had turned a corner too fast and literally bumped into Joel. Her packages had scattered everywhere, and one of her shoes had gone flying into the air.

As they struggled to retrieve their belongings, Joel had looked up from his position on the ground and flashed her that flawless smile, extending her missing shoe to her.

Despite her indignation and embarrassment, Samantha had started to laugh, but not before some shaken-up synapse in her brain registered the fact that this man had the most fantastic smile she'd ever seen.

"Earth to Samantha. Earth to Samantha. Darling, where were you just now?" Joel teasingly asked, interrupting her reveries.

"Oh, I was just thinking how we first met. You literally knocked me off my feet!" She laughed, giving him an affectionate poke in the side.

"Oh, yeah? Who got knocked off their feet? You came around that corner hell-bent-for-leather. After the crash, I remember thinking you were the clumsiest Cinderella I'd ever met!"

"And I recall hoping you weren't really a frog underneath that princely exterior!" she quipped.

"Everything's going to be fine, Sam—as long as we keep our sense of humor and our loyalty to one another." Joel guided the car expertly around a foul-smelling bus.

"Absolutely essential," Samantha agreed, smiling. As always, she was more than grateful that she had married Joel.

Oh, there had been a stream of men who had flowed through the doors of the apartment over the years, but none of them were made of Joel's stuff. He'd also been the only one who'd made the effort to discover the real woman beneath Samantha's bright bubbliness.

"Home at last!" Joel cried triumphantly as he swerved the little car into the narrow driveway lined on each side with tall, stately fir trees.

He switched the ignition off and swiveled around to plant a kiss on Samantha's cheek. "Want to come up and see my etchings?"

She nodded quietly, suddenly overcome by the awareness of how rich her life was. Joel came around to help her out of the awkwardly fashioned car and they walked, arm in arm, up the flagstone walk to the two-story Cape Cod house. Authentically shingled in gray clapboards with contrasting white shutters, the dwelling was a piece of New England in the Midwest.

Samantha remembered the excitement she'd felt after she and Joel bought the house. Although, as a son of an Army colonel, Joel had lived in a series of different houses over the years, Samantha's only version of home was the city apartment she and her father had shared. She'd never had a yard before, never planted a garden. She'd never hosted an outdoor barbecue. Life in suburbia was different—and good.

Joel turned the key in the lock and they stepped into the foyer, snapping on lights before they entered the living room. "I'll hang up your coat," he said.

He helped Samantha shrug her way out of her taupe Chesterfield and she went into the blue-and-camel-colored living room. Above the white, painted mantel of the fireplace was a seascape set off by matching brass whalers' lamps on either side. Wing-backed chairs, Queen Anne tables, and a high-backed sofa graced the rest of the area. A Persian rug was bordered by the polished sheen of hardwood floors. Nearly all of the furnishings in the house had been passed on to them by Joel's widowed mother, who, after her husband's death, had put everything she owned in storage and then traveled around the world. When she had eventually moved East to live in a small, chic apartment, she'd shipped her treasured possessions to Samantha and Joel—as a wedding present.

Joel came up behind Samantha and circled her waist with his arms. She leaned back against him, resting her head against his shoulder. "I love this house," she said softly.

"Aha!" Joel cried. "The truth at last. You did marry me for my exquisite taste, my incomparable wealth, my—"

His words were cut off as Samantha whirled suddenly in his arms and went directly for the sensitive area under his ribs. Long fingers tickled his midriff unmercifully. A slender hand groped for his belt buckle.

Laughing, Joel put up only the mildest resistance. "I hope this is leading where I think it is," he murmured against her creamy cheek.

The tickling stopped abruptly. Samantha threw the belt to one side. "Let's go upstairs," she whispered.

"I surrender," Joel answered huskily.

They climbed the carpeted stairway slowly, arm in arm. As they entered the master bedroom, Joel bent over to switch on the gentle light of an electrically lit candle sconce. Soft light spread over the white, carpeted floor, highlighted the sheen of the cherry armoire, vanity table, and the four-poster bed. The deep rose of the satin coverlet and drapes blushed prettily against the same subtle hues of the striped wallpaper.

Joel pulled Samantha's lean body against his. Two shadows splayed across the wall in the filtered light. He tilted her head back and kissed her. It was a movement without obvious passion—gentle, calming, and strangely arousing. A sense of desire so strong that it sent tremors through her body gripped her.

"Let's take it slowly, Sam, darling," Joel murmured. His voice was low, huskily confident, filled with the promise of wonderful moments. "You feel so good." His hands cupped her face and then slid down the regal lines of her neck to the base of her throat, resting lightly against the pounding pulse above her breastbone.

Then his fingers moved back up to the perfect oval of her face, tracing the slight pout of her mouth, the short straight nose, and the delicate tissue around the enormous blue eyes. From there they caught in the cloud of golden hair that had earlier been secured in a neat topknot.

Samantha matched the lazily arousing pace of his movements. Her hands roamed unhurriedly over the vibrating cords of his bronzed neck, on up to the square, clefted chin, along the high-set cheekbones, to the dark, winging brows.

Her eyes, midnight blue, locked with Joel's. In the dimly lit room, his eyes seemed almost black with desire.

Joel's fingers continued to trace their way upward beneath her sweater. He still hadn't touched her skin, only the thin cotton of the blouse she wore. Idly he traced each rib, until she felt his warm probing on the undercurve of her breast. It felt heavy, throbbing with her need of him. As if in a slowly moving dance, Samantha swayed, fitting herself into the curve of his arm, bending against him so that his hand cupped the lush fullness of one breast. The nipple swelled under the kneading manipulations of his fingers and her heartbeat tuned to the insistent rhythms of desire.

Joel spread her golden cascade of hair across her shoulders. He buried his lips in it, teasing the sun-bright tendrils until they fell away from her earlobe. Then he turned his attention to the pink shell of her ear, his teeth nipping lovingly at the sensitive skin, his quick, warm breathing echoing the thudding in her chest.

"Oh, God, Samantha, I want you," he groaned.

Samantha was savoring the slow, insistent attentions of his lovemaking, and like a child putting off the first delicious taste of a favorite treat, she took her time raising her arms above her head.

Joel caught her hands, lifting them to pull her sweater over the shining mass of golden hair. Then he deliberately unbuttoned each pearl stud on her blouse, watching her flushed face as he did so. In seconds the garment lay discarded on the floor, along with her sweater.

Strong fingers reached behind her and unclasped the sheer, lacy French bra. Her large, creamy breasts tumbled free of restraint, exposed to his reverent, dark gaze. Samantha arched her back in an agony of expectation and Joel responded immediately, lowering his lips to the rigid, rose-colored nipple of first one breast, then the other.

"Beautiful. Too much for one man to deserve," Joel gasped, wetting the tip of his finger and circling each tumescent bud lovingly.

"Joel," Samantha pleaded, "let's go to bed."

He swept her into his arms, her silky hair a halo against the rough blue wool of his sweater. Laying her gently down on the bed, he knelt over her, catching her lower lip between his teeth, nibbling it tenderly, the way one cherishes a delicacy. Samantha clasped his face between her palms and carefully forced her tongue into the innermost recesses of his mouth.

They gasped at the mutual pleasure of her exploration. And then with the naturally catlike grace bestowed by his rangy frame, Joel lowered his body onto the bed to lie beside Samantha.

"Undress me, Sam," he said, the rasp of his voice betraying his urgency.

She rose to her knees and quickly set about the requested task. With fingers made skillful by passion and practice, she eased his sweater over his head. Carefully, she undid his Oxford cloth shirt, one button at a time. Her hands crept beneath the waistband of his flannel pants, playing gently along his flat, muscled abdomen. A sharp intake of breath greeted her shameless exploration and her hands flew to the zipper. In seconds, the pants lay over the small valet chair by the bed.

She nuzzled her lips against Joel's hard nipples, running her hands delightedly over his curling chest hair. When her fingers lowered to his inner thigh and on to the growing evidence of his desire, he lay for a moment, basking in her rapt absorption, and then turned over to unzip her slacks.

His hand moved beneath the filmy nothingness of her

panties, seeking and finding the throbbing pulse that filled her with a fiery longing. Through a haze of desire, Samantha moved to the tempo of his deliberate strokes. Soon his fingers were replaced by his lips and she shuddered with wild pleasure. Joel slid her panties and slacks down her long, bare thighs and over her feet.

All vestiges of control vanished and Samantha placed her hands on Joel's shoulders. "Please, darling." Her voice sounded as if it came from the depths of her soul.

He planted his palms on either side of her and slowly, tantalizingly, slid his body the length of hers until he lay fully on top of her, the weight of his chest burning into her aching breasts.

She arched her curving hips into Joel's rock-hard leanness and then, swept away by the force of the mutual power they wielded, she guided the warm, gliding pulse within her. Joel closed his hand over one sumptuous breast, subtly caressing the budding tip until it stood proudly away from the surrounding flesh. He bent his head, taking the nipple in his mouth. Pulling and tugging with his lips and tongue, he savored each musky taste.

The incredibly stimulating ministration of Joel's mouth and the rocking rhythm of their hips caused Samantha to gasp. "Joel!" she cried. "I love you. Ah, darling, don't stop. Please don't stop!"

"Never," came the husky reply. "Never, Sam. Not until—" His voice broke off as Samantha gripped his muscled buttocks to drive him deeper inside. Together, they crested wave after wave of fierce, pounding desire.

Carried away, transported to a wonderful haven where all of her fantasies were fulfilled, Samantha forgot herself as she merged with Joel. She was both the possessor and the possessed, a woman vividly and lovingly released from the constraints of reality. When the final, shimmering ecstasy traveled the length of their bodies, she pulled Joel's head to her shoulder, letting the cocoon of silky sweetness completely envelop them.

They lay, legs entangled, between this semi-conscious

state and that of true sleep. Samantha was dimly aware of Joel's still-rapid breathing, his mouth pressed into the curve of her cheek, his dark hair against the tangled mass of her own golden tresses.

"A penny for your thoughts," he whispered against her damp skin.

She stirred, nestling him closer against the fragrant hollow of her shoulder. They had been discussing something earlier. What was it? That disturbing little voice in her head was desperately trying to nudge her saturated senses into proper thought, but Joel's comforting nearness silenced it.

"I love you," she whispered sleepily and snuggled closer to him, the nagging pinprick of thought lost in the oblivion of total fulfillment.

— 3 —

"HOLD THE DOOR, Sam. That's it. Okay, now it's your turn." Joel wedged his leg against the heavy door to keep it open for her. Samantha maneuvered past him into the hall, balancing a grocery bag on each hip. Joel, his arms similarly laden, followed, cursing softly under his breath. "Damn! Probably bought too much again! But you can't ever be sure..."

His voice trailed off as Samantha staggered to the butcher-block work island in the sunny kitchen and promptly let go of the bags. Their contents spilled everywhere.

"Great!" she cried. "Oh, what a mess! I'm weaker than I thought."

Joel placed his bags carefully on the counter and turned around to survey the mess. "Maybe I should have joined the Army, like my father. That way, we could have had delivery service," he teased.

"You didn't have your groceries delivered, did you?" she asked, surprised.

Joel looked at her. "Sure," he said. "Lowly non-coms used to beg for a chance to deliver a colonel's groceries."

"I see." Samantha nodded gravely. "I'm married to a thirty-year-old Army brat."

"Oh, yeah?" Joel challenged, his dark eyes gleaming with mischief.

Samantha feigned horror, covering her mouth with her hand, taking tiny steps backward.

Joel advanced slowly. "Private!" he boomed in his best General Patton voice, "I'm assigning you K.P. duty

25

for your insubordination—effective now—eighteen-thirty hours!"

Samantha clicked her heels together, gave a sloppy salute, and began to hum, "The Army Goes Rolling Along." She'd hit only two wrong notes when Joel pulled her to him, cutting off her words with a kiss.

As he released her, Samantha stood at attention again. "Begging your pardon, sir, but that kiss was not appropriate. After all, I'm only a private . . ."

Joel rested his hands on her slender shoulders. "Then, private, perhaps we should do something about your rank. Perhaps a change of uniform would help . . ." He kneaded her upper-back muscles suggestively.

"Later." Samantha laughed, ducking to escape the tempting pressure of his fingers. "Right now, darling, I've got to pick up the mess I made and get to work on the party preparations."

The huge shopping binge had been in preparation for Joel's office party, which Samantha had offered to give this year. She bent and began scooping up the scattered groceries.

If there weren't so much to do before tomorrow night, she would have loved to continue their little game. Joel's high spirits and sense of comic relief were two of the reasons she was so drawn to him. As an only child, she'd whiled away the hours of her father's absence by watching romantic comedies on television—or inventing her own fantasies. The result was that she loved good, old-fashioned horseplay, and Joel entered into the charades with enthusiasm. Often their games blended into the foreplay for ardent lovemaking.

"So, you're not interested in trying on the uniform the Army reserves for special occasions?" Joel asked despondently, giving her an I-know-where-it-could-take-us look.

Samantha arched a golden brow. "Oh, I'm definitely interested, darling, but what about all of this work?" She gestured toward the piles of unwashed vegetables, the packages of raw hamburger, and the bag of unboiled noodles. "You're the one who said we need to get as much of this as possible done tonight!"

"Did I say that?" Joel slapped his forehead. "Me and my big mouth! But you're right, Sam, I'd better get to work on the sauce for my pasta. We'll save dessert for later—regrettably."

"It will give us something to look forward to," she said slyly. "Don't expect me to lather whipping cream on my head, though!"

"You're getting awfully conservative in your old age," Joel teased, opening a broom closet and donning an enormous apron that had the words "Chief Bottle Washer" spelled across its front. Samantha watched him out of the corner of her eye. It was a tribute to Joel's masculinity that the female garment seemed only to enhance his sex appeal. Stretched tightly across his broad chest and narow hips, the hem rested discreetly on his thighs.

Get to work, Samantha, she told herself. Keep your mind on cleaning these damned vegetables!

Joel dashed around the kitchen, tossing noodles into a pot of boiling water, grating cheese, and browning hamburger. In between chores, he shoved groceries in cupboards.

"Is everyone coming tomorrow night?" Samantha asked, whisking a pile of scrubbed-clean radishes into a plastic bag.

"So far as I know. It should be a great party. If we get most of the preparation done tonight, we can just relax and enjoy ourselves."

Although the party was for Joel's office staff, they'd invited a few neighbors, too. Samantha loved being hostess at such functions. They were fun, and they gave her the opportunity to see her husband in a different light. He was a charming host, at ease, thoughtful, witty. He had the ability to draw people out, to make them talk excitedly about their lives. His buoyant enthusiasm served to convince them of their importance to him, so why not to themselves? Anything seemed possible when Joel lent his encouragement. Samantha suspected this quality was responsible for much of his business success.

He had gotten in on the ground floor of the video games industry, starting Hyperspace with a healthy bank loan and his savings from a previous job with an insurance company. Six years later, he'd paid off the mortgage on the building, as well as the equipment. He then instituted a profit-sharing plan, and as a result, his employees were both hard-working and loyal.

Moving from place to place with the Army had made Joel able to deal well with social situations; it gave him an exterior polish that seemed to have deepened his self-confidence as well. A lesser personality might have succumbed to shyness and self-doubt when denied geographical roots, Samantha thought. But Joel had used his kaleidoscopic background to advantage.

Samantha twisted the top off a bright orange carrot and applied the vegetable scraper to its pitted skin. Oh, yes, she knew a lot about Joel, just as he did about her. They were a "closed corporation" in many respects, confiding their innermost feelings only in one another, preferring their shared companionship to that offered in large, noisy outings...

"Sam, there's not going to be anything left of that carrot if you don't stop scraping it," Joel warned.

"Hmmm? Oh, yeah. Well, I'll save it for Miss Davenport. She eats like a bird anyway." Samantha turned from the sink. "You're sure you don't mind my inviting her, Joel?"

"Of course not, honey. I've told you before, I had a grandmother just like her—not an ounce of tact in her old body, but it was all a front for a soft heart underneath that iron-clad bossom." Joel chuckled.

Samantha smiled. Miss Davenport did possess caring instincts, but in performing an act of kindness she usually preferred to masquerade her charity in the guise of businesslike transactions. This knowledge of the old lady's fundamental character had worked in Samantha's favor shortly after her father died.

She and Joel had tried keeping Watson at the house, but he'd run away so much, Samantha had gotten desperate. She suggested to Miss Davenport that she live rent-free in her family's apartment in exchange for taking care of Watson. This had proved satisfactory to everyone involved. Now the secretary was close to her job, instead of having to ride the bus across town, and Watson was safely happy in his old environment. Although Miss Davenport wouldn't admit it, she loved having a companion—someone, as Joel often put it, as manipulative, arrogant, and independent as she was!

"Well," Samantha said, "I just hope my sprightly secretary's in a good mood for the party."

"Who do you think you're kidding, Sam? Miss Davenport's *never* in a good mood."

"Now, darling, she has her good days and her bad. When Dad was alive and feeling well, she was really quite different. Of course, she had lots of work to occupy her mind then," she added wistfully.

"Honey," Joel said quietly, laying down his spatula, "every business has its problems. You're not alone in that, you know."

"But I owe it to Dad—and to myself—to make the agency successful again, Joel. It'll have benefits for you, too. You know as well as I do that modern marriages succeed more often if both partners are fulfilled in their work."

Joel frowned, the heavy, black brows arched like birds in flight. "Come on, Sam. That sounds like a quote from one of those insipid magazines you've assured me you never read."

"It's my *own* quote, Joel," Samantha said firmly. "And I'm absolutely right. If my business fails, I'll end up hanging around at Hyperspace, annoying everyone!"

"I won't let you," Joel promised, crossing the room to lay his hands on Samantha's shoulders. "Besides, you can't even type—and I already have a perfectly good secretary."

Samantha stiffened under his caress. What was the matter with him? He could usually read her moods so well, easily distinguishing the serious from the transitory. Never had he sloughed off her concerns so casually before. She was beginning to get the distinct impression he wasn't really interested in whether the agency's business improved or not.

When she had still been in the overwhelming grip of grief over her father's death, Joel had been there for her. He had even taken time off from Hyperspace to help with the funeral arrangements. Afterward, he'd continued to listen, comfort, and reassure.

Although Samantha knew she couldn't begin to equate her present troubles with her father's death, she was, nevertheless, bothered by Joel's seeming refusal to share her disappointment in her work. This careless attitude was so unlike him. He'd been a strong supporter of her independent and—admittedly—unorthodox profession since before they were married.

She took a deep breath in an effort to control her rising anger. This issue had to be resolved before it took a serious toll on their relationship. Two patches of color appeared on her cheeks and her voice shook slightly as she spoke. "Joel, I am not an incompetent, nor am I some dope who thinks she's a female version of Philip Marlowe. But I know what I know—and that is, I'm very good at my job! I'm beginning to think, however, that you have no faith in my ability."

For a moment, Joel looked as if she'd struck him. His dark eyes turned opaque and he raked a hand feverishly through his hair. Stepping away from her, he walked over to the work island and leaned heavily on it.

Samantha stood watching him. She knew she'd strained the cords of their mutual support system with her pointed accusation. Her heart was torn between wanting to go to him and wanting to walk out of the room. Finally, she whirled around and went back to scrubbing the vegetables in the sink. Minutes ticked by on the large kitchen clock, the steady beat growing louder and louder in the tension-charged silence.

Then she was aware of Joel's hands on her hips, his breath whispering at the delicate nape of her neck. "Turn the water off," he commanded in a low voice.

Automatically, she pushed at the faucets. His hands moved from her hips up the sides of her lean midriff. Even through her heavy Irish wool sweater, Samantha could feel the rotating pressure of Joel's fingers, gently massaging her sides, moving slowly but deliberately up and around toward the generous undercurve of her breasts. She found herself anticipating the moment when he would touch the swelling flesh, lift his hands to relieve the aching tenderness.

Joel seemed to sense her need and, pressing himself closer to the swell of her buttocks, he brought up his hands to cup each breast, his fingers seeking out the well-defined nipples.

Slowly, and then with gathering urgency, Samantha's hips began to rotate in an unmistakably yearning message against the pressure of Joel's thighs. He moaned gently into her ear, teasing the lobe with his lips. And then, a violent burbling sound exploded through the mist of her desire, causing her to go rigid.

"Damn!" Joel swore. "The pasta sauce! Just let me turn it off. Stay where you are!"

Samantha felt his hands leave her body as he crossed to the stove and she slowly turned from her position at the sink. What was the matter with her? She was about to go to bed with a husband *who hadn't even said he was sorry*. She reminded herself she was a grown woman, twenty-six years old, mature enough to know there were lots of ways to apologize. But she couldn't accept sex as one of them—at least not this time.

Joel removed the pot from the burner and started back to her. The look on her face stopped him dead. "Something tells me that in between here and the stove, we've lost touch," he said carefully. He stood in the bright light of the Tiffany lamp in the kitchen, obviously wounded. A telltale muscle in his cheek twitched signs of anger, too. Stubbornly, he shoved his hands deep into his flannel slacks and shot her a fierce look. "Sam, I don't like arguing with you. We've always been so close. This is ridiculous."

"Isn't it?" she said coolly.

Joel bent forward a little, studying the gleam of the tiled floor. When he raised his head, Samantha saw with alarm that he appeared exhausted—Joel, who usually seemed the epitome of energy with his Cary Grant looks and his bronzed coloring!

Chastened, Samantha went to him in a rush, throwing her arms around him. "Joel, darling, you look so tired. Are you feeling okay?"

He buried his lips in her neck for a moment, his lean frame relaxing against hers. "I'm fine, Sam. Look, honey, I'm sorry I've behaved badly. That usually isn't my style. Let's forget it for tonight, huh? We can discuss the whole thing later."

She traced the angular lines of his face, running her finger lovingly along his jaw. He was just tired, that was all. Better to drop the subject of her professional future for now. "Sure, darling. Let's finish up here and have a sandwich in front of the television. We can build a fire and take it easy."

She was rewarded for her conciliatory efforts by Joel's heart-breaking smile and a playful swat on the bottom. "You're on, lady! Race you to the finish line!" he cried, sounding more like the old Joel again.

Hurriedly, they finished putting the lasagna casseroles together and wrapped them carefully, placing the Pyrex pans in the freezer. Samantha handed Joel the scrubbed and bagged vegetables to store in the crisper, and he put the dirty dishes in the sink to soak while she made bologna-and-Swiss-cheese sandwiches.

"I'll go make a fire, Sam. Why don't you put those sandwiches on a tray with a nice bottle of wine and join me?" Joel lifted his eyebrows up and down, Groucho Marx fashion, and Samantha laughed delightedly.

"Save my place," she commanded.

Minutes later they settled onto the floor with their backs resting against the sofa in the firelit den. The flames threw off orange and blue shadows that flickered across the cozy room. Joel had tuned the television to an old "Thin Man" movie, one of Samantha's favorites.

Balancing his tray carefully on his lap, Joel took a bite of the thick sandwich Samantha had made. "Hmmm... This is good stuff, Maynard!"

"Gourmet delights are my specialty, sir." Samantha raised her glass of wine and added, "To the master chefs. May we continue to cook in unison!"

Joel clicked his glass against hers. "Always," he said softly.

Samantha managed a smile over the brim of her wineglass and then looked into the fire. *Always*. Joel and she had successfully survived the earlier tension in the kitchen, but she realized they'd merely applied a salve to their wounds. The injuries they'd inflicted upon one another weren't healed. Never before had there been a problem they couldn't work out, but this time...

Joel had always supported her in everything. He was not only her best friend, but also her helpmate and lover. And she'd returned his loyalty. Now, when she particularly needed his enthusiasm and understanding, he'd let her down, disappointed her in the worst way by making her feel he had no faith in her abilities or in the goals she'd set for her business. The agency was such a vital part of her life. She'd thought Joel understood that. Why wouldn't he dig in and help her sort out her frustrations? Offer some concrete advice?

"Whew! That was a close one!" Joel exclaimed. "It's lucky for Nora that Nick's arriving to bail her out."

Samantha turned her attention back to the black-and-white images flashing in front of her. Nora Charles, the female half of the famous detective team, was confronting a bullying criminal in a deserted warehouse. The whole situation was tense, fraught with danger, but Nora was relying on her verbal expertise to stall the man. And now it appeared Nick had arrived with the police.

Samantha spoke before she thought. "It's nice that Nick can be depended on in a crisis." As soon as she'd uttered the words, she realized their possible misinterpretation by Joel. Would he think her casual comment was intended as a pointed reminder of their earlier argument?

Joel looked over at her, his face patterned in subdued shadows. He was so handsome, he took her breath away. The aristocratic lines of his face were highlighted in the dancing flames and his eyes glowed the color of chocolate, except for remarkable green rings around the pupils. Great! Samantha thought. Most women had husbands who ranged from ordinary to above average in looks, but she had one who made her heart feel as if the blender was set on puree!

With tender amusement, she started to reach out for Joel, but he laid a restraining hand on her arm. "I thought we agreed to drop things for now, Sam," he cautioned. "Let's not start something neither of us is prepared to finish tonight."

Exhaustion, confusion, and frustration were all taking their toll on her. Communication had always been a strong point of the marriage, but short of screaming she didn't know how to reach Joel tonight. Actually, the urge to discuss her goals for the agency wasn't so important to her as Joel's attitude. Something was wrong. And for the first time since she'd met Joel, he appeared unwilling to delve into the heart of the matter.

She made herself mentally count to ten before she spoke. "I think we'd better turn in, Joel. I'm really tired and I want to be fresh for the party tomorrow evening."

If either Joel or Samantha noticed her use of the phrase, "turn in," instead of "go to bed," neither one acknowledged it.

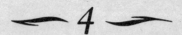

4

SAMANTHA FROWNED INTO the cheval mirror in the bedroom. "Bad choice, Sam," she said to her seductive reflection. "This is what comes from buying a dress on your lunch hour without taking the time to try it on."

Twirling around slowly, she saw that her worst suspicions were confirmed. The halter top the saleslady had referred to as "modified" was anything but. "'Abbreviated' would be a better term," Samantha muttered aloud.

The dirndl skirt of the blue silk was in reality a narrow piece of material slit to the thigh on each side. The nipped-in waist was practically nonexistent because of the plunging back and front that left little material to gather around the middle.

"Great! I look as if I bought the whole darned thing two sizes too small!" she wailed.

"Whoa!" Joel drawled as he came into the room. "Good Lord, Sam, what's happened to your cashmere sweaters and designer slacks? Is this a new image?" He walked slowly around her, taking in the ample curve of her scarcely confined breasts, the shapely thighs, and finally the smooth expanse of her bare back.

Samantha crossed her arms over her chest and then turned serious. "Joel, what am I going to do? You know how I hate to shop. This is what comes from impulse buying—nothing! I mean, I look as if I have nothing on! I can't even wear a bra with this stupid outfit!"

Joel ran his hands over her arms, his eyes raking her graceful, silk-sheathed curves. "I like it," he pronounced.

"You look absolutely smashing, Sam! I can't wait to show you off. All of you," he added slyly.

Samantha looked at him in exasperation. "For Pete's sake, Joel! Don't you think I ought to change? I can take the dress back tomorrow." When he didn't respond, she waved her hands to gain his attention. "Joel! Are you with me? This dress is a gorgeous color, but there's so little of it and—"

"And I love it," he interrupted, gripping her bare back. "I absolutely love it," he repeated, feathering kisses down the side of her jaw, onto her neck, then her shoulder, leaving burning trails of fire on her skin.

Samantha caught her breath. How was it possible that Joel could always divert her attention with a caress, a touch, a kiss? She forgot the dress as his hand slid to a breast, skimpily covered in the sheer fabric. The velvety nipple thrust demandingly through the material, sending ripples of desire up and down her lithe body.

"Joel, darling," Samantha pleaded half-heartedly. "The guests—"

"Won't be here for a few minutes yet," he answered huskily. "Ah, you feel so wonderful, Sam. I can never get enough of you." His hand moved from the front of her dress to inside and, as his fingers closed over her bare flesh, Samantha hoped the party guests would all forget to come. Her sense of propriety, her intention to finish tossing the salad, and her plans to check on guest towels all flew out the window.

She was aflame with longing. When Joel raised her skirt, pushing aside the thin strip of bikini panty to seek the moist center of her desire, she moved her hips frantically.

"Yes, Sam, that's it. Oh, I want you—"

The shrill jangle of the phone on the nightstand shattered the moment. "Damn! Who in the hell can that be?" Joel cried.

"Do we have to answer it?" Samantha sighed, her breathing coming in irregular gasps.

"Damn!" Joel swore again. "I'll get it, love. I'll be right back. Don't move!"

Samantha sank onto the bed and feebly smoothed the folds of the silken skirt. She took a deep breath and hoped fervently that the caller would hurry and get off.

Joel yanked the phone from its cradle. "Hello," he barked into the receiver. He listened for a moment and then his voice became businesslike. Turning his back to Samantha, he spoke in murmured tones.

From her position on the bed, she could catch only snatches of the conversation. "Looks as if that's the case? I was beginning to wonder— Finish checking and let me know the outcome tonight. No later."

Wordlessly, Joel replaced the receiver and walked to the dresser. He stood in front of the mirror aimlessly brushing his thick, dark hair.

Samantha rose instantly from the bed. "Is there a problem, darling?"

"A snafu at work," he answered tersely, straightening his tie by giving it an overly vicious yank. Beneath the smartly cut suit jacket, his shoulders were hunched tensely and he stood with his feet spread slightly apart. There was a menacing quality to both his stance and demeanor.

Samantha had never seen this side of Joel. If she'd ever hoped his peculiar reactions of late would simply dissipate, she knew now she was wrong. Starting across the room to him, she stopped suddenly as the peal of the doorbell echoed through the house. "Oh, my gosh, Joel! Somebody's here! Can you get it, darling? I'll be down in a minute."

"No problem," he answered smoothly, giving her a perfunctory kiss on the cheek as he went out the door.

Samantha stood for a few seconds staring after him. She couldn't remember Joel ever kissing her so briefly— so emotionlessly—before.

Samantha stood in the living room chatting with the accountant from Hyperspace. As she made the appropriate responses, her eyes swept over the guests. The party was going well. Dinner had been served and now people were clustered in small groups, laughing and sipping after-dinner drinks. Even Miss Davenport in her prim navy suit appeared to be enjoying herself.

Joel was sitting by the hearth with Brad. Their conversation seemed animated and her husband more like himself. Samantha considered this more carefully as she continued to nod and smile at the accountant. He was relating a long-winded story about his former employment in a C.P.A.'s office.

Joel, she mused, appeared normal again, but how long would it last? He was relaxed, himself, until something or someone closed in on him, demanding his full attention. Then he withdrew behind a veil of casual indifference, or close-to-the-edge anger. She had no way of knowing if he'd been this way with his employees, too, over the past few days, or only with her. Pride and loyalty to Joel prevented her from asking anyone.

Joel saw her watching them and signaled for her to come over.

"Excuse me," Samantha apologized to the accountant.

Brad looked up with undisguised admiration as Samantha joined them, standing to kiss her on the cheek and offer a chair. "Wow! That's some dress, Samantha! I'm surprised you'd let your wife appear in public in that, Joel!"

Samantha winced inwardly as she sat down, but managed a radiant, if slightly crooked smile. "Joel's the one who suggested I wear it tonight," she said sweetly.

Don't be paranoid, she rebuked herself. But she felt the old currents of uneasiness arise. Brad's sexually laden comments could be so annoying! Deep down she wondered if she were just jealous of Brad. After all, he was Joel's closest friend, and Samantha knew Joel had plans to make Brad a full partner in Hyperspace before long. Used to sharing nearly everything with Joel, it was hard for her to accept that Brad filled a part of his life she couldn't. She didn't understand computers, and that was just the trouble!

But there was more to her discomfort around Brad than a few suggestive remarks, she acknowledged for the first time. She remembered the time when she and Joel had hosted a touch football game in their spacious yard. Brad had managed to graze her breast or slide his hand up her thigh . . . Of course, those things often happened in the heat of a game, so she had no real reason to suspect they were anything out of the ordinary. Did she?

"It's really a dynamite dress, Samantha. Joel has good taste," Brad said generously.

Joel smiled easily, motioning for Brad to rejoin him on the hearth. "After all, I was smart enough to hire *you*, Brad."

Brad chuckled, his blond mustache turning up to expose a set of flawlessly white teeth. Samantha smiled. Did the city of Minneapolis put something in its drinking water to ensure that its citizens had smiles that lit up rooms?

"How come you didn't bring a date tonight, Brad?" Samantha asked.

"I told him to," Joel said solemnly. "But I'd guess Brad didn't want to be encumbered by a lady tonight. He probably wanted to make it an early evening, since he's getting ready to leave on vacation tomorrow."

Brad clapped Joel affectionately on the shoulder. "It's getting harder every year to maintain my macho image," he said. "You've found me out."

Both Samantha and Joel laughed. "You're doing just fine," Samantha said. "I don't know how you keep all of those women's names straight!"

"Okay! Enough joking about my entangled love life!" Brad warned good-naturedly. "Now if I could only meet someone like Samantha—maybe I'd be able to settle down."

She shifted in her chair uncomfortably. Take it as a

compliment, dummy, she told herself. It's just more of Brad's banter. He's so used to flirting, he can't play it straight. Smoothly, she replied, "Oh, Brad, I find that hard to believe. A carefree bachelor like you? Why, the world's your oyster!"

"Oh, off and on," Brad said easily. "More off than on lately. It's true, I am slowing down in my old age!"

Joel reached for Samantha's hand. "Well, my friend, when you finally come to a complete stop, I hope you're as lucky as I was."

"Here, here!" Brad replied cheerfully, tipping his glass and draining it. "Well, I probably ought to be making tracks. I still need to get a few last-minute things together for the trip."

"Where are you going, Brad?" Samantha asked curiously.

"Don't know exactly where yet—but someplace sunny and warm! I'm hanging loose until tomorrow. Then I'll make up my mind...That's one of the joys of being a bachelor, you know. I have only myself to please."

Brad lit a cigarette, inhaling deeply, then blew the smoke out in a thin, blue stream. "I wasn't really due to take vacation until next week, but Joel said the other day that I could go ahead and leave as soon as I got organized."

Joel stood, putting an arm around Brad's shoulders. "You deserve a break. You've been working hard lately. Best thing in the world for you is to find some sun and relax completely! Come on, I'll walk you to the door."

Brad bent to kiss Samantha's cheek. "Thanks, Sam. I enjoyed myself, although I always leave here feeling envious. You and Joel make marriage look so appealing!"

Samantha smiled. "Glad you could come, Brad. Have fun on your vacation!"

As Brad and Joel made their way to the door, Samantha sat staring into the fire for a few seconds. Then, remembering her duties as hostess, she returned to her guests. Circulating among them, she chatted easily, then noticed that several glasses needed refilling.

Hurrying into the kitchen, she found Miss Davenport stacking dirty dishes in the sink. "Miss Davenport! You don't need to do this! Joel and I will take care of it later."

"Never does to put off until tomorrow what can be done today, Samantha," the old lady retorted fiercely.

Samantha bit her lip to keep from smiling. "I thought I'd send some leftovers home with you—for you and Dr. Watson to share."

"I don't need any, but that piggish cat would love them. He was very upset about my leaving tonight. Probably dumping the wastebasket out of spite this minute! The food will be a peace offering."

"No doubt," Samantha answered. "You can always placate Watson by filling his tummy."

As she wrapped goodies in neat, foil packets, her mind wandered back to the phone call Joel had received earlier. He'd said there was a snafu at work. She didn't doubt that. There were always complications in the video games industry, but Joel's reaction to this particular problem had bothered her. She'd never seen him strung so tightly before. Nor had he ever dismissed her concern in such a terse manner.

Something was very wrong. Whatever it was had profoundly affected their lives over the last few days. Joel faded in and out of his normal personality as if he were an actor trying new roles on for size . . .

With a loud cluck of her tongue, Miss Davenport finished rinsing the dishes. "There! All ready to go in the dishwasher. No more mess!"

Samantha put her arm around the elderly woman. "Thank you. I appreciate your help. You're a loyal friend." For one emotional moment, Samantha considered blurting out her worry about Joel. But she decided against it almost as soon as the thought crossed her mind. The old lady was already squirming uncomfortably, embarrassed by Samantha's display of affection.

"Always try to be a help, I say," the secretary said,

moving out of Samantha's embrace to swipe at a dirty glass she'd missed.

Yes, Miss Davenport did, in her own way, attempt to offer support. But she was not the kind of woman whose shoulder one cried on, the type who invited emotional confidences. Taking a deep breath, Samantha said, "Thanks for doing the dishes. Now I really must get back to the other guests."

"Do that, dear. I've called a cab and I'll be leaving soon anyway. Don't neglect your guests."

Samantha shot Miss Davenport a parting smile as she picked up a tray of liqueurs and headed back into the living room. Joel was standing in a corner talking earnestly to two of Hyperspace's programmers. His face was grimly set, his mouth compressed into a thinly drawn line. Apparently, he'd lost not only his host's affability, but his good humor as well.

Puzzled, Samantha started toward the trio. Halfway across the room, she was interrupted by several guests who needed their glasses refilled, and when she was finally able to put the tray down on the coffee table, Joel and the two men were gone. Maneuvering her way skillfully through the downstairs rooms, she nodded and smiled at people, her eyes anxiously searching for Joel. But there was no sign of him.

An hour later, the party started to break up. Samantha was helping sort out coats for departing guests when Joel appeared at her side. "Hi! Have you been lost in the shuffle, darling? I've looked everywhere for you," she said lightly, handing their next-door neighbor her fur jacket.

"I—I had to go outside for a while, Sam. Sorry."

The tone of Joel's voice disturbed her, but he pasted on a party smile and joined in ushering the guests out the door. One of the last to leave was a man who lived down the block and loved to brag about his bachelorhood. Obviously a bit tipsy, he leaned toward Samantha, his eyes fixed pointedly on the curve of her breasts above the thin, silken top. "Loved your party," he slurred. "Not to mention your dress."

Joel grabbed the man quickly by the arm and shoved him out the door. Samantha gasped. Never before had Joel behaved so jealously! For one thing, their obvious love for one another seemed to discourage others from making passes, and for another, Joel seemed confident of Samantha's reaction to such rarely proffered overtures. His trust and faith in his wife had carried him smoothly through awkward situations until now.

As the final "good night" was uttered, Samantha grew so eager to talk to Joel privately that she nearly closed the coat hem of Hyperspace's accountant in the door. Apologizing, she waved him on down the walk and then turned anxiously to Joel.

"What is it, darling? What's the matter?" The words came out an octave higher than usual.

Joel walked over to the sofa and sank down heavily. His face was ashen and his usually sparkling eyes were dull with worry. "I've got a problem, Sam," he said simply.

What kind of problem? The little voice inside her head was shrill. Samantha went to him immediately, kneeling down and taking his hands in hers. "Tell me about it," she pleaded.

"Remember my telling you about working on a new game—Catwalk?"

"Sure. Your brainchild."

"I can't find it, Sam. It's missing. I kept thinking there was some mistake, but tonight two of my best programmers told me they'd finished checking out not only my terminal, but the mainframe downstairs, too—and there's no mistake. Catwalk has been deleted from the computer's memory. Undoubtedly the thief stored the program on a disk, and then erased all record."

Shock registered across Samantha's features. "Someone *stole* your idea?"

"Exactly."

She stood up and began to pace around the room. "You have no idea how this happened, Joel?"

He shook his head and his thick, dark hair fell in his eyes. "No. At first, I thought maybe I'd screwed up, programmed my idea incorrectly, accidentally erased it— whatever. But," he added tiredly, "the simple fact is that Catwalk's been stolen."

"Industrial sabotage," Samantha breathed.

Joel passed a hand across his face. "I suppose so."

Suddenly, Joel's erratic responses of the last three days seemed entirely explainable. But Samantha didn't dwell on that. Her professional instincts were busily surfacing. "What does this mean to your company, Joel?"

He looked at her grimly. "Strictly speaking, it means someone has an idea in his or her hands that is potentially worth a great deal of money. Sam, you know half of making it in this video industry is beating your competitor to the punch—marketing your idea first. Catwalk is a very hot concept, a sure money-maker."

Samantha knit her golden brows together in concentration. "You hadn't finished refining it, of course." Not waiting for a response, she plunged on. "But it was far enough along that somebody with the right kind of expertise could. Is that right?"

Joel punched absently at a bolster pillow on the sofa. "Yes. Of course, whoever stole the program for Catwalk is going to have to market it, solicit a buyer, as well as find somebody who'll refine it. Reputable representatives of video game companies are not going to deal with the thief—at least not openly. The least investigation on their part should make it clear the idea came full-blown from another concern— There are ways of telling such things, too complicated to go into right now. But anyway, the guilty party will probably try to sell to someone dishonest, or perhaps someone who is having financial difficulties and needs a hot merchandising gimmick."

Unanswered questions kept popping into Samantha's mind. "How do you know the thief doesn't have the ability to utilize the best parts of the game or even to complete it—and then sell it to someone, passing it off as his own idea?"

Joel looked startled. "Well, that's partly what I meant before. For one thing, nobody with that kind of expertise has access to my computer. It would be impossible to get the source code listing. We have our own kind of security checks at Hyperspace, Sam—" His voice broke off and he stared down at the rug.

"Joel," Samantha said impatiently, "who does have access to your private computer? Who knew about Catwalk?"

When Joel lifted his head, his eyes were haunted. "My secretary—Mary Beth—Brad, and myself."

Samantha expelled her breath. "So—we're talking about only two possible suspects, aren't we?"

Joel didn't answer.

"Joel?"

"I suppose so." It was a simple response articulated with the heavy tones of distress.

Samantha moved onto the sofa next to Joel. "Darling, I'm sure this is a stupid question, but why can't you recreate Catwalk and hurry up and market it—beat the thief to the punch?"

Joel massaged his temples. "Because, Samantha, it was an inspiration, one of those ideas that comes to you in a fevered pitch, like the concept for a song or a story. Recreating Catwalk would take a lot of time—although it could be done . . . but there's more to the situation here than that."

He gripped the edge of the coffee table, his knuckles whitening with the exertion. "I have to know why somebody would betray me. Loyalty is a quality I prize and I thought I knew when I received it in return. Evidently, I've made an error in the judgment of an employee's character."

Samantha's heart went out to Joel. He was so intrinsically honest, operating with his own high standards of integrity, expecting others to reciprocate... "Joel, what are you going to do?" she asked quietly.

He leaned back against the sofa cushions, pinching the skin between his heavy, black brows with his forefinger and thumb. When he finally spoke, his voice was hard, tinged with underlying fury. "I don't know yet, Sam, but, believe me, when I find out who betrayed me—and why—there's going to be hell to pay!"

Samantha reached out to touch Joel, but he rose quickly from the sofa. Scooping up a glass on the coffee table, he hurled it with uncompromising force into the wall. "I'll clean that up myself, later," he muttered, stalking from the room.

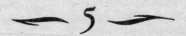

— 5 —

SAMANTHA TOSSED RESTLESSLY in the king-size bed and then stretched her hand out to touch Joel. Her fingers met the cool expanse of sheet instead of his warm flesh. She sat up and peered at the clock on the nightstand. Three in the morning! Pushing long strands of golden hair from her face, Samantha leaned back against the pillows and sighed.

In the six months they'd been married, she had never before felt so powerless to comfort Joel. He had been betrayed. Such an experience would be a shock for anyone, but to Joel . . . well, his code of honor simply couldn't accept such a thing. Proof of that was that he'd attributed the loss of Catwalk to human error until he'd finally had his computer checked by the programmers.

Yet Samantha knew that Joel, with his razor-sharp intelligence, must have suspected, deep down inside, that someone other than himself was to blame for the loss of Catwalk. Perhaps he hadn't at first, but by the second day he must have unconsciously been thinking in terms of sabotage. Reflecting back, she remembered how he had grown so upset, so emotionally evasive over the smallest confrontation.

With each passing day, he'd moved a little farther from the personality to which she was accustomed. He'd given away bits and pieces of himself to placate her, while the whole man must have been moving rapidly toward this inescapable conclusion.

It would do no good to ask Joel to admit this. In fact,

he probably wasn't aware of it, even now. Apparently, though, he had made a decision not to share his distress with her. Why? To her knowledge, he'd never kept anything of consequence from her before.

And then the answer to her question hit her like a bolt of lightning: She'd been too wrapped up in her own frustration over the agency to pursue the reason for Joel's odd behavior. No. That couldn't be the explanation—not the sole one anyway. Joel was more self-assured than that. He also had more respect for the mutual understanding in their marriage, the confidence that, had he discussed the seriousness of his problem with her, she would have dropped everything to comfort him.

So why had he hidden his concern from her? Why the secrecy? Getting out of bed and putting on her blue velour robe, Samantha shoved her feet into the matching mules and went downstairs. She found Joel in the kitchen, hunched over a cup of coffee at the oak trestle table.

"Hi," she said softly.

He looked up, his features strained even in the mild light of the single-bulb fixture above the table. "Sam, what are you doing up? Did I make too much noise?"

She sat down next to him and lovingly stroked his cheek. "No, of course not. Sitting and brooding doesn't exactly resemble the loud cheers of a high-school spirit squad, Joel."

He gave her a feeble smile. "I'm sorry about throwing the glass, Sam. But I cleaned it up a while ago. No damage to the wall."

She took his hand. "I'm not worried about the wall, Joel. I'm worried about you—or us, I should say. Why didn't you tell me about the loss of Catwalk as soon as you found out?"

Joel knew Samantha's question demanded and deserved a straightforward response. "I wanted to protect you. You've had a rough adjustment to your father's death and I didn't want to upset you—especially over what might have turned out to be nothing."

He paused and rubbed his hand absently over the stubble of his unshaven face. "After the programmers called—before the party—to tell me they were in the process of running complicated tests to determine whether the computer's machinery was faulty, and that so far the results had been negative, I wanted to tell you. But the doorbell rang; we were interrupted, and then . . . somehow, the moment had passed . . . If wanting to protect you was patronizing or arrogant or chauvinistic—I'm sorry as hell, Sam!" he continued. "But I love you— and I thought this whole damned thing might blow over. Hoped to hell it would."

Samantha frowned, her blue eyes fixed pointedly on his face.

"But you're right, darling," he admitted. "I should have confided in you. Instead, I behaved insensitively toward you on occasion. I didn't mean to . . . I just couldn't seem to concentrate. Except when I held you in my arms, made love to you—those weren't pretend situations. Those were real—and my salvation."

Samantha closed her long-lashed eyes with relief. "Thank you for telling me all of this, Joel. And as for wanting to protect me—well, I suppose I'm flattered." She smiled to soften the effect of her next statement. "That is, as long as you don't make such an error again."

"I love you," Joel replied quietly, looking into turquoise depths to see his emotion reflected back at him. "I love you very much."

"Me, too," Samantha said gently. "Now, darling, back to Catwalk—"

"Right. Oh, Lord, Sam! I don't know what to do about confronting Mary Beth. She's the mother of two children, for Pete's sake!"

"Joel," Samantha countered firmly, "being a mother doesn't necessarily mean you're a candidate for sainthood!"

Joel rose wearily from the table and poured himself another cup of coffee. "Want some?" he asked.

"Sure."

Joel brought the two cups of steaming liquid back to the table. "Sam, I think I'll call Mary Beth."

"Now?"

Joel's eyes focused on the bright, sun-faced clock above the stove. "Uh, no, I suppose not. I'll wait." Absently, he spooned sugar into his coffee.

Samantha took a deep breath and placed her hands in front of her on the table. "Joel, why do you suspect Mary Beth only? Brad had access to your private computer, too."

Joel swished his spoon angrily around the cup. "Good Lord, Samantha! Brad's my oldest friend! He's more than just an employee!"

She had expected this reaction, so she was able to control hers. "Joel, you must be more objective. Mary Beth is simply not the only one who had access to that computer!"

Joel stiffened, but remained silent.

Samantha tried again. "Honey, after you talk to Mary Beth, we'll be in a better position to evaluate this situation. Let's not quarrel over who makes a better suspect now. Okay?"

He nodded and looked away from her, out the window into the dark, fog-shrouded night. Samantha felt as separated from him as if she were still upstairs sleeping alone. An old expression of her father's came back to her—*jumping from the frying pan into the fire*. She glanced at Joel. His face was a carefully composed mask, and she had no idea how to close the gap between them.

Samantha glanced at the kitchen clock—eight in the morning! Five strained hours had passed. She'd tried going back to bed, but had been unable to sleep without Joel by her side. So she'd gotten up and busied herself by performing countless little household chores.

Joel was just hanging up from his tactfully worded conversation with Mary Beth, his face registering conflicting emotions. Closing the door to the dishwasher quietly, Samantha walked over to him.

"I forgot," he said simply.

"Forgot what, darling?" she asked gently.

"I forgot that Mary Beth went to the dentist the day before yesterday."

Samantha was desperately trying to fit this piece of information into the puzzle, when Joel smiled grimly. "You see," he continued, "I spent all morning working on the game. She left for her appointment while I was still in my office." He ran a hand through his already tousled hair.

"She had a root canal. Later she called to say she wouldn't be in until the next day. In fact, she's still experiencing pain—asked me to apologize to you for not making the party."

Samantha put a hand on Joel's arm. "But did she perhaps return from the dentist when you were out? She could have sneaked into your office, you know. Think, darling. When were you gone from your computer during the day?"

"Let's see . . . I had lunch sent in. Brad joined me. Then he went back to his own office and I worked for a while longer."

Joel began to pace around the kitchen, his fingers pressed to his brow. "I was having some difficulty debugging Catwalk. So I decided to take a breather. I went to the lounge downstairs, drank a can of soda, and then returned to my office, sat down to work on Catwalk, and couldn't retrieve it. That bothered me, but I figured I'd fouled up somehow—was suffering mind blight or something. That's when I decided to leave early, come get you . . ."

He stopped walking and leaned against the sink. "I ran into Brad in the hall and we walked out to the parking lot together. Then I drove straight to the agency—no! I take that back. I had to run an errand. I'd promised John Beckett, one of the programmers, that I'd drop a new manual by his house. I really just wanted to be with you—get to the agency as fast as I could. But I'd given John my word and he'd been in bed all week with a cold, so—"

"You kept your word, of course," Samantha said admiringly. How like Joel! He was always conscious of fulfilling promises, living up to expectations, even to the extent of foregoing his personal welfare sometimes. She smiled, gathering her courage to ask the next question. "Did you mention your problems with Catwalk to Brad?"

Joel looked at her blankly, then shook his head. "No. I really figured it was still human error that was the problem. Brad doesn't know much about computers or their programming—at least in their technical aspects. Marketing's his game. Besides," he added bitterly, "I didn't want to ruin Brad's vacation with what might turn out to be a simple case of panic."

"And so you didn't talk to him about Catwalk last night?"

Joel raised his eyebrows. "Sam, I didn't know anything for sure until after Brad had left the party. Remember? The programmers came to the party late—straight from the office—to give me the bad news. That it hadn't been a technical error, after all. The game was gone—stolen."

Samantha did remember the sequence of last night's events, but she was rapidly slipping into her professional manner and careful repetition of known facts was part of that. "Had you tried to retrieve Catwalk yourself, at the office yesterday?" she asked, pressing on.

"Yeah, a couple of times. But I didn't have much opportunity. Brad and I were tied up with those computer salesmen all day. We were so busy listening to their spiels, taking them to lunch, touring the facilities with them—I figured I'd just have to leave my problems with Catwalk until today...But I *thought* about the situation plenty. Every time there was a lull in the conversation or a repetitious pitch I'd heard a million times before, my mind wandered back to Catwalk."

"I'm sure it did, darling. You really haven't been yourself lately—and now I understand why." Samantha tapped at her chin with her finger, an old habit she slipped into when she was trying to concentrate. Wishing she could think of some bit of reassurance for Joel, she squeezed her eyes tightly shut and willed herself to come up with something—anything that might be helpful.

An idea made its way into her sleep-starved mind. "Call the dentist, Joel. It's nearly nine. He'll be there by now."

His dark brows lifted quizzically. "Call *who?*"

"Mary Beth's dentist. Did she mention his name? If not, we can find out. It's simply a matter of—"

Joel interrupted her. "She did tell me his name in the course of the conversation. Dr. Whitman." The light of understanding crossed his face. "Hand me the phone book, Sam—please."

She pulled the phone book from the counter drawer and Joel rapidly flipped through the pages, running his finger up and down the W's until he came to the listing he wanted.

A few seconds later, he'd completed the call. Hanging up the receiver, Joel's dark gaze met Samantha's. "Mary Beth was in the chair until after five o'clock. The dentist had an emergency and she had to wait. That's why she called me earlier, to tell me the whole afternoon was shot as far as working was concerned. I just didn't pay much attention to the particulars of the explanation."

Samantha was shocked to feel a guilty satisfaction course through her. She'd always liked Mary Beth and, although her profession had taught her criminals were often the least likely suspects, she'd had a gut feeling that Mary Beth couldn't be responsible for the theft of Catwalk. The woman had been in the dentist's chair during the time the game had disappeared. *Brad. Brad had to be the thief.* Silently, she waited for Joel to voice his suspicion of his friend's treachery.

When he didn't, she put her arms around him. "Darling? You know the obvious now. What are you going to do?"

He started as if she'd pinched him. Dark eyes, usually lit by humor or kindness, reflected black fury. *"Why?"* he asked, making a visible effort to control his anger. "Why in the hell would Brad pull something like this? We're best friends! And although I hadn't told him yet, I planned on making him a full partner in Hyperspace next month. He should have known he could count on me... None of this makes sense!" Joel moved away from her and reached for the phone.

Samantha stood helplessly by while Joel dialed Brad's number repeatedly, receiving no answer. He hung up and sank into a chair. "I'm calling the police," he stated emphatically.

Samantha sat down across the table from him. "And tell them what, Joel? That Brad might have gone on vacation? That he might have skipped with your game— for whatever reasons?"

He leaned forward and rested his weight on his elbows, staring past her. "I don't know."

"Joel," Samantha said patiently, "you don't have any real proof that Brad is the thief. Everything points to it, but we have nothing concrete."

Joel didn't look up as he spat out his response. "That worthless ingrate! What in the hell could have been his motivation? We've been friends for over fifteen years— and he turns on me!"

Her heart constricted with pain for Joel. "My experience with the criminal mind has been that motivation for illegal acts runs the gamut, darling. Perhaps," she ventured softly, "Brad has never been the kind of person you thought he was."

Joel slammed his fist down on the table. "How could I have been wrong about him? And how could he have been so wrong about me?"

Her eyes clouded with confusion. "What do you mean?"

Joel raised his head and met her startled gaze. "What I mean is—how could he have figured I wouldn't come after him? He knows me better than that. I intend to find him if it takes me to the other side of hell and back! Farther, if necessary," he added in an angry, determined voice. She'd never heard him use quite that tone before.

Of course! She might have known Joel would never let a matter of treachery lie unavenged. That kind of forgiveness was not in his nature. He was uncompromising when it came to the issue of loyalty. His father had imbued the entire family with his unwavering code of honor, trust, and truth. Part of her had married him for those very qualities...

And then some marginal synapse in her brain made an overdue connection. She could take Joel's case! Not only would she be helping her husband, but also herself. This was a chance to prove her mettle, to use every bit of knowledge she instinctively possessed, as well as all she'd learned from her father. If she could find Brad and the missing game, she would be able to satisfy Joel's furious bewilderment over why a trusted friend had betrayed him. She would also be taking the first step toward giving the agency a full spectrum of cases once again!

"Darling," she said excitedly, "I'll take your case!"

He couldn't have looked more surprised if she'd told him she planned on running off with the circus. "Sam," he began falteringly. Then his shoulders straightened and his voice took on a firmer tone. "Sam, I don't think that's such a hot idea. It could be dangerous, for one thing. For another, industrial sabotage is big-time stuff. It's not as simple as, say, catching a guy in bed with someone other than his wife! And what if Brad has gotten in with a really rough crowd?" He shook his head. "I don't want you involved in anything like that."

Turquoise eyes turned a glacial blue. The voice that usually had the lilt of a songbird went flat. "Danger, as you well know, has always been part of my job. It comes with the territory. And, as for your allusion to 'big-time stuff,' I want to remind you I'm a professional, Joel."

"It's *my* problem, Sam. I'll handle it myself."

Samantha's lower lip jutted out and she smacked the smooth finish of the table with her palm. "Since when have we had his and her problems, Joel? I thought when we got married we agreed we'd be a team, sharing all our concerns."

"This is different, Sam." Joel's voice was cold and hard.

"It's only different because you choose to make it so. I want to help you. I know I'll be able to solve this case!"

Joel rose abruptly from the table. "Do you want a ride downtown?" he asked, his voice frosty with ice.

Samantha sat at her desk in the agency attempting to concentrate on some paperwork that needed to be done. Miss Davenport had taken Dr. Watson out for his daily "airing." Upstairs in the apartment the grandfather clock chimed melodic sounds, signaling the middle of what had been a very long afternoon.

Rising from her desk, Samantha rubbed the back of her neck. She was suffering from an incipient headache, tense muscles, and a heartache she figured to be roughly the size of Texas. The discovery of Joel's utter lack of faith in her professional abilities, his disdainful dismissal of her offer to help him, his cool distance from her in the car that morning—all of these had both wounded and angered her.

She was considering kicking the desk when the door opened and Joel walked in. Samantha's heartbeat quickened as she was caught in a vortex of conflicting emotions. Part of her wanted to hurl herself into Joel's arms, but the other part—the proud, stubborn streak inherited from her father—caused her to cross her arms over her full breasts and fix a glare on him befitting Bette Davis playing Queen Elizabeth.

Joel eyed her nervously for a few seconds before removing his coat. Pivoting on one foot, he turned around to give Samantha a full view of his back. She gaped in amazement for a moment and then her full lips began to lose their regal pout. A muscle twitched uncontrollably in her cheek and a small chuckle escaped her lips.

"Wait! You haven't seen the best part yet!" Joel cried, reaching into his pocket for a small tin. Quickly, he smeared the charcoal-like substance it contained on his face and then, hunching his shoulders and bowing his head, he approached his wife.

As he stood before her, a gunnysack tied around his shoulders, patches of charcoal on his forehead, cheeks, and chin, Samantha shook her head in disbelief. "What do you think?" he asked humbly. "Contrite enough?"

She stared at him, her eyes wide. "Sackcloth and ashes! Oh, Joel, honestly..."

His penitent pose vanished as he swept her into his arms. "Sam, I'm sorry, honey. Will you accept my apology?" His lips nuzzled her neck, her throat, slid back up to her mouth, nibbling tentatively... A deliciously warm feeling crept into her limbs. She kissed him back with fervor, oblivious to the charcoal smudging her creamy skin.

As they drew slowly apart, Joel put his hands on her shoulders, searching the depths of her blue eyes. "Apology accepted?" he asked huskily.

"I guess I'd be a fool not to," Samantha answered breathlessly.

Joel smiled with relief and reached out to fuss with the comb that still held her tumbled, blond curls, albeit precariously. "Sam, I've been to the police. You were absolutely right. At this point, a private detective is what I need."

"Got anybody in mind?" she asked softly.

"Yup. A tall, good-looking blonde with the biggest blue eyes this side of the Mississippi. Is she still available?"

"Hmmm . . . If she agrees to take you on immediately, will she appear too easy?"

"Not to my way of thinking."

"Okay!" Samantha cried delightedly. "Joel, I really am good at what I do. You didn't know Dad or me when the agency was hopping, but we actually handled all sorts of cases. That's how I was able to earn my investigator's license so easily. I had the experience, you see—"

"Whoa! I believe you, Sam. You don't have to convince me of your competency. I know that for a fact. It's just hard for me to admit I need help, I guess, because I never expected to be in this situation. But I appreciate your offer and I want to take you up on it. Can you forgive me for being such a stubborn jackass?"

Samantha smiled radiantly. "Of course. I think we've both been overreacting, darling. You have to expect it in a tense situation like this, especially where feelings are involved." She turned to her desk to pick up her pad and pencil. "Let's see, there are lots of things I need to sort out. I think I'll start with—"

She was stopped short by the emphatic look in Joel's eyes. "Not *I*, Sam. *We*."

"*We?*" she repeated incredulously.

Joel nodded. "Yes. I can afford to take some time off from Hyperspace to help with the investigation. It only makes sense that the two of us work together, Sam."

He looked past her out the window at the traffic below. Then his eyes, reflecting his inner turmoil, shifted back to her astounded face. "I *have* to be personally involved in this case, Sam. There's no way I can sit back and relax until Brad is caught—until I confront that—" He paused, attempting to find a description adequate to express his wrath. "That treacherous creep face to face!"

Samantha puffed out her cheeks, letting the air escape in one dramatic exhalation. "I suppose you know I don't think this is a good idea."

"I figured you might feel that way, Samantha, but you have to consider my side, too." Joel studied the tip of his loafer. "I need the personal satisfaction of catching him, exposing his treachery. Look at it as an emotional catharsis—whatever—but I've got to be part of this investigation."

She understood Joel's reasoning, but she felt morally obligated to explain to him why it was less than a good idea. "Joel, you aren't objective enough about this situation to help me investigate. And you don't have the credentials. What's more, I think it'll be too emotionally painful for you to be involved."

He made a sound of disgust, then his face suddenly softened. "Sam, you're the one who said we should share our concerns, operate as a team. Are you going to take back those words?" His voice was a honeyed plea.

She winced. Joel was too darned sharp. He was also the man she loved with all her heart. Exposing him to the full extent of Brad's treachery—whatever that might be—well, the thought was unbearable. Yet there was no mistaking the glimmering determination in those dark eyes. She felt like a lottery winner who'd misplaced her ticket, hoping desperately to find it, but knowing if she did, the results might be more than she'd bargained for: If she tried to keep Joel off the case, she would be risking the harmony of their relationship—and if she didn't, the result could be the same.

"All right," she said reluctantly. "But you've got to promise to let me run things my way, Joel. I'm the detective. You're not."

"I promise," he said solemnly, and then he broke into a broad smile, the smile that always had such power over her . . .

Sighing, Samantha deliberately looked away from her husband's perfect teeth. She was committed to this unorthodox investigation now. Her father would turn over in his grave if he knew she were allowing a nonprofessional—and a close relative, at that—to aid in solving his own case! And what would Miss Davenport say? Plenty, no doubt. Oh, boy, you've got yourself a case all right! she reproached herself.

Joel interrupted her thoughts. "Better wipe the charcoal off your face before Miss Davenport comes in," he cautioned.

She reached up and touched her cheek absently. "Yes, I suppose so. Might as well have a clean face now— because when she gets done with me, I'm certain to have egg all over it!"

— 6 —

MISS DAVENPORT WAS in the process of confirming Samantha's worst suspicions. "Joel belongs in Hyperspace, Samantha. He has no business interfering in this agency! It's not professional, not productive, and not necessary! He'll only be in the way." The old lady huffed over to her desk. "Furthermore," she continued, "I thought you had more spunk than to allow your husband to try to protect you from your own profession!"

Those words hit home. Miss Davenport had honed in on the most sensitive of Samantha's fears: Was Joel insisting on being involved in the investigation so that he could baby-sit her? She felt a raw, bubbling anger at such a possibility. Yet she couldn't be sure. Joel was, by nature, honest. If his underlying motive was the desire to protect her, it was probably because he hadn't even admitted it to himself—yet. Perhaps his grievous anger at Brad's deception was manifesting itself in overly possessive behavior. It was possible that, unconsciously, Joel now feared losing everyone dear to him.

I'll just have to wait to see how this goes, Samantha thought. Joel had been so pleased about her agreement to work with him that she had seen some of the tension of the last few days literally drain away. He appeared more relaxed and last night . . . Last night had been wonderful! They'd made the skillful, consummate love only two people totally in harmony with one another could enjoy.

"Are you listening to me, Samantha?" Miss Davenport barked.

62

Wearily, she nodded. "Yes, and you're no doubt right. But I'm going to *try* working with Joel. We made an agreement."

Miss Davenport raised her eyebrows. "Did he sign the standard contract?"

"No, he did not. At least not yet," Joel answered loudly as he came in the door of the agency. "But he will."

Samantha looked helplessly at Miss Davenport and then at Joel. "You don't have to sign a contract, darling," she protested.

Slipping an arm around her shoulders, he said firmly, "Oh, yes, I do. I insist. I want to be a paying client who fulfills his contractual obligations to the letter."

"Joel, this is ridiculous," Samantha countered.

Miss Davenport had already inserted a document in her ancient Underwood. "He's right, Samantha," she corrected. "If he insists upon being a part of this agency's business, then he can sign our standard contract." She began to type furiously.

Shaking her head in disbelief, Samantha bent to stroke Watson, but the cat, almost as if he had an uncanny perception of the circumstances, rolled over on his back and played dead. "Swell!" Samantha moaned. "My cat thinks he's a dog; Joel thinks he's a detective; Miss Davenport imagines herself to be head of this agency—what am I? Chopped liver?"

Joel grinned. "Are those rhetorical questions, Sam? Or do you expect us to answer you?"

"Spare me," she pleaded, half-seriously.

Miss Davenport unrolled the paper from the typewriter and handed it with a flourish to Joel. "Sign here," she said crossly.

Joel complied, then, looking triumphantly down at the tiny woman, asked smugly, "Now is everything in order?"

"You ought to read things before you sign them," she

answered haughtily and snatched the document from Joel's hand, marching across the room to file it in the rusting cabinet by Samantha's desk.

Samantha realized it was time to make a hasty exit. "Let's go, Joel. We need to get started. Time really is of the essence."

"Okay, darling," he mumbled absently. Then, unable to resist a parting shot, he called out, "Have a nice day, Miss Davenport. And you too, Watson!"

Both the cat and the secretary ignored the couple as they scurried out the door.

Half an hour later, Samantha and Joel arrived at Brad Davies's bank. "Let me do the talking, darling," she instructed as they entered through the main entrance. "And no matter what, follow my lead."

Joel nodded solemnly. "Right."

They stood looking around for a few moments before Samantha crossed to a window nearest them. She and Joel waited their turn. When the teller looked up expectantly, Samantha's bright smile wavered.

"I need help," she said, her tone one of utter desperation and despair. She glanced at Joel, ignoring his incredulous stare.

The teller squinted at her from behind horn-rimmed glasses. "What kind of help, miss?"

Samantha leaned as close to the man as the restraints of the window allowed. "It's sort of personal," she whispered.

"I assure you that our loan department operates on a purely confidential basis, but I'm not in charge of that sort of thing. Let me take you—"

Two irridescent teardrops slid down Samantha's cheeks. "Oh, no, I don't want a loan." She gulped. "I need help in locating my boyfriend. At least I *thought* he was my boyfriend. B-but now I don't know what to think. He's disappeared."

The teller took in Samantha's weeping countenance,

her full, trembling lips, and the intoxicating scent of her perfume. "Uh—please, miss. Surely, things aren't as bad as they seem."

"Worse," Joel said, failing to disguise the sarcasm in his voice.

Samantha turned around and shot him a reproachful look. "Excuse me," she apologized to the teller. "This is my cousin. He came all the way from Schenectady to be with me. You see, I've been so upset—"

Ignoring Joel, the teller said softly, "I can see that. But how may I help you? I want to, of course, but I don't see what I can do."

"My boyfriend is Brad Davies, an account holder at this bank. He's always spoken so highly of your institution," Samantha lied, "that I knew you'd be able to help me. I can't find Brad! And he owes me money—not a tremendous sum, but enough that—"

"I'm sorry to hear that," the man at the window commiserated. "I do know Mr. Davies, and I must say I'm surprised—and sorry—"

"It's a real tragedy," Joel agreed, attempting to look sympathetic, but his expression seemed rather to fall somewhere between patronizing and phony.

Samantha sniffed loudly. "Can't you give me a little information? I just need to know if he still has an account with this bank. I need that money he owes me. I've got bills to pay, you know—"

"Especially with family circumstances being so hard," Joel elaborated, his eyes shining with mischief. "There's Uncle Tim's operation and—"

"Yes," Samantha interrupted hastily, pressing a tissue to one tearing, blue eye, but managing to glare at Joel out of the other one. "I do have many obligations. Not only do I want the money owed me, I want to find Brad, talk to him—find out why he left me—"

"High and dry," Joel supplied.

"Yes. Exactly," Samantha said. *"Anything* you can tell me will help. I'm at a loss as to what to do."

The teller blinked. Samantha sniffed.

"Well," the man began, "it's strictly against bank policy, but if you promise—"

"Absolutely. I'd be so grateful. Much more grateful than I can express in words," Samantha added, lowering her thick, dark lashes.

An hour later, Samantha sat munching a German chocolate doughnut in a bakery a few blocks away from Brad's bank. Joel sat across from her, a cup of coffee before him. He shook his head. "I still don't understand why you think we know anything more than we did, Sam. I'm confused, I guess. Your ruse did work with the teller; he talked to us, but I honestly don't know what he told us that was so important."

Samantha carefully removed a flake of chocolate from her upper lip. The procedure at the bank had gone smoothly and she was feeling pretty good about it. In an effort to keep things light, she said teasingly, "Yours is not to reason why—"

"Ah, Sherlock, that's where you're wrong. As a *paying* client, I deserve to know everything."

Wiping her hands on the paper napkin that lay in her lap, Samantha lifted innocent blue eyes to her interrogator. "Well, first of all, I could tell a lot by the teller's reaction when I told him my story about being dumped by Brad. He was sympathetic, and I knew if I played my cards right, he'd tell me *something.*"

"I was hoping you wouldn't have to lay down any aces," Joel commented sarcastically.

"Second," Samantha continued, ignoring his remark, "after I'd finished making him feel sorry for me, I let him do most of the talking. People always tell you more if you remain quiet and let them carry the ball."

Joel arched a heavy brow. "Was it really necessary for you to introduce me as your cousin from Schenectady, who came to help you through your hour of heartbreak?"

Samantha cocked her head mischievously at him.

"What did you want me to introduce you as—my husband?"

"You've made your point."

"I thought so. Now, when I told the teller how desperate I was to get in touch with Brad—"

". . . he finally said how very sorry he was, how he had always thought of Brad Davies as a responsible, fair man." Joel paused and looked uncertainly at Samantha. "He went on to tell you Brad withdrew all of the money from his checking and savings accounts. And he also said there wasn't a lot of money in either account and that he wished you every success in locating Brad. That he wished he had a forwarding address, but that he didn't . . ."

Samantha nodded, her face flushed with excitement. "Exactly. Oh, Joel, don't you see? Brad must be in deep financial trouble! He makes good money with your company. So why wasn't there more money in either account? As I see things, Brad was *driven* to steal Catwalk."

Joel expelled his breath. "Nonsense, Sam! You're jumping to conclusions! Maybe Brad has another account with some other bank or savings institution. We still don't have any real information to use against him—or even to help us find him!"

Samantha bit disgustedly into the last of her doughnut. Swallowing hurriedly, she said, "Joel, I certainly plan to check to see if Brad has—or had—any other accounts. But we needed to start somewhere. If you find this so tedious, perhaps you should—"

Dark eyes challenged hers.

"Perhaps you should—have another cup of coffee, and try to relax," she suggested lamely.

"I don't think more caffeine is the answer to my tension," he replied tersely. Then he smiled. It was an effort, Samantha realized, to keep the peace between them.

"No, I suppose not," she said evenly.

A tension-filled pause drifted between them. Suddenly, Joel's dark brows shot up quizzically. "Say! How did you know which teller to pick?"

Samantha tipped up her milk glass and drained it. "Elementary, my dear Watson. You said Brad always ran errands on his lunch hour, but not during the usual twelve-to-one slot because he liked to avoid crowds—at the cleaners, the post office, the *bank*. Brad took his lunch hour from one-thirty to two-thirty."

"So?"

Samantha ran a finger around the inside of her empty glass. "According to the signs posted by each teller's window, only three of them are normally open between those hours. And two of them were clear at the other end from the main entrance. If Brad were in his usual, efficient hurry, I figured he'd probably pick the closest teller, that is, provided that our man, Mr. Simpson, didn't have a long line of people waiting for his services. It was really sort of an educated guess, darling, nothing more . . ."

Slowly but surely, Joel's face shone with grudging admiration and then he burst into laughter. "You're something else, Samantha Loring! I'm beginning to think you're either damned good or damned lucky!"

She knew she should have been angry at his refusal to give her an unqualified compliment, but for some reason, she wasn't. "Call me anything, just don't call me unreliable," she sang in a slightly off-key soprano.

She was so caught up in her comical performance, she didn't notice the look that came over Joel's face. "That's a promise, Sam," he answered huskily, reaching across the table to cover her hand with his own.

Samantha responded immediately to Joel's touch. A tingling excitement coursed through her, but she knew that once she had mentioned the next step in the investigation, that thrill would be taken away. For a moment, she allowed herself the luxury of drowning in Joel's darkly intense gaze and then stood up quickly. "Time to get going," she said, more lightly than she would have imagined possible. "We need to pay a visit to Brad's house."

Samantha untangled her cramped frame from Joel's sports car and stretched in front of the two-story colonial house. Swinging her arms high above her head, she brought them to rest at her sides and turned to face Joel, who was leaning against the hood of the car watching her. The wind ruffled his hair, arranging the shiny, dark strands in seductive disarray.

There was a speculative look in his eyes. Samantha wondered if he was thinking of Brad or her. The trip to the house had been made in silence and she had been unable to think of anything reassuring to say. She knew he was afraid of what they might or might not find. So, for that matter, was she.

How strange this all was! She and Joel, each of whom could often verbalize what the other was thinking, somehow found no words to communicate at all, no mutual thoughts to discuss. As they stood with their eyes locked on each other, Samantha felt as though she were observing the physical attributes of a stranger: the lean, hard thrust of Joel's jaw, the strong, clefted chin, the chiseled lips . . . Electricity charged the air.

She forced herself to break eye contact with Joel, telling herself they must get down to business. The sooner this was over, the better. Adopting an air of nonchalance Katharine Hepburn would have envied, she asked, "Shall we look around?"

"I'll ring the bell first," he replied impassively.

They walked side by side, but not touching, up the flagstone path to the house. Large evergreens obscured the front windows so that it was impossible to see inside. Joel punched the doorbell several times and its eerie echo reverberated in the wind.

Samantha suggested they walk around back.

"Are you talking about breaking and entering?" Joel asked.

"Darling, we need to find out what's going on," Samantha explained patiently. "Maybe—just maybe—Brad is inside."

The almost imperceptible slant of Joel's mouth told her he saw through her thin excuse. "You don't believe for one minute he's in there, Sam. You're looking for clues, not him."

"Whatever," she said briskly. "At any rate, we must search the house. If you don't want to be part of this, Joel, why don't you wait in the car?"

He shoved his hands stubbornly into the pockets of his trench coat and narrowed a hard gaze on Samantha. "Don't you think there are better ways to go about this? Going to the bank is one thing, but Brad's house . . . Not only is this against the law, but I fail to see what we'll gain by sifting through Brad's personal things. I don't need to do that to know he's guilty!"

Joel looked away from his wife's glowing skin, her perceptively knowing blue eyes. Damn! he thought. She sees right through me. I'm not worried about the police or the illegality of this, only my reaction to being in Brad's house again. We shared so many good times together here—laughing, talking, partying . . .

Samantha stood waiting for Joel to wrestle his way through his emotional entanglement with Brad. His personal sensitivities were shadowing his objectivity. He was attempting to tell her how to conduct her business. And he was suffering real pain. None of this would be happening if it weren't for his hard-nosed insistence on being part of the investigation.

Firmly, she replied, "Joel, if there were a better way to handle this, believe me, I'd know. Our only other option is to present substantial evidence to the district attorney so a search warrant can be issued. Now—unless you're holding out on me, the only evidence we have is circumstantial." She paused, hoping he would buy this explanation for the need to enter Brad's house. It would be less distressing for Joel to think she assumed he didn't understand investigative procedure than for him to realize she knew he was caught up in a painful bank of memories of a once-trusted friend.

"Okay," Joel mumbled. *Thanks for the out, Sam,* he wanted to say. But some foolishly prideful streak kept him from admitting his gratitude.

"Joel, if you want to change your mind, it's okay, you know. I tried to warn you that this job wasn't as safe and exact as, say—a computer business. The hours are irregular, there are risks, and there are times when waiting for a break in a case can get pretty boring—"

"Spare me the speech again, Sam! Please. I'm not changing my mind. We're in this *together!*"

She depended upon a light retort to serve her better than a serious one. Rocking back on her heels, she drawled, "Yup, partner, it's you and me—all the way into the sunset."

Joel, who was usually a sucker for her Dale Evans's act, did not respond. He stood lost in thought on the porch of Brad's house until Samantha was forced to say, "Joel, it's getting late. I think we ought to jimmy our way inside and look around, before it gets too dark to see. If we have to use a flashlight, we're liable to draw attention, the kind that can mean accompanying someone wearing a uniform, downtown."

Storm clouds were beginning to build up and the sun's brilliance faded into an eerie, gray light. A shadow crossed Joel's face. "Okay," he said simply.

How badly she wanted to comfort him! He was so shaken by Brad's disloyalty that the darkness of his disillusionment was coloring their lives together. As she dug into her shoulder bag for her lock pick, Samantha considered telling Joel this wasn't necessary, that they could go home—that he should be spared the anguish of entering Brad's personal environment. But the little voice inside her head told her that to do so would be not only unprofessional, but would also bring them no closer to the solution they needed so badly in order to get on

with their lives. Yes, it was definitely something that
had to be done.

The door opened easily and they entered the spacious
living room. As they moved through the downstairs rooms,
Samantha expertly checked closets and the drawers of
the built-ins along the living room and family room walls.
She even looked beneath chair and sofa cushions, carefully replacing each one. Finding nothing of consequence, she led the way upstairs. Joel trailed silently
behind her, offering no advice.

Samantha routinely repeated the search she'd made
downstairs, entering and leaving each room with a pre-
cise efficiency. Joel hung back. Finally, he sat down at
the top of the stairs and began to whistle an old, maudlin
Irish tune. Samantha ignored him and headed into the
last second-story room, her heart pounding furiously with
an emotion she couldn't quite identify.

Was it guilt? Or was it worry over Joel's response to
this whole situation? Whatever, she didn't like the feeling. Throwing her head back in determination, Samantha
started to search what was obviously the master bedroom,
a part of Brad's house she'd never been in before.

The walls were a subtle shade of blue, set off by white
woodwork. She stood in the center of the room, turning
slowly around. Recessed lighting tracks ran along the
stenciled molding that separated the walls from the ceiling. Her feet sank into the deep, dark blue plush car-
peting, shadow-patterned by the translucent light of the
approaching storm.

The king-size bed, with its blue-and-white flame-
stitched spread, seemed to mock her, as did the sleek
white dresser and chests. This room was having a powerful effect on her. There was an almost embarrassing
aura about it. She felt as if she'd walked in on Brad and
a lover.

Clenching the fullness of her lower lip between her
teeth, Samantha forced herself to go quickly through
Brad's drawers. Nothing! Then, trembling slightly, she

opened the louvered doors to the huge walk-in closet. Empty! All of Brad's clothes were gone! He couldn't have taken everything in his wardrobe on a vacation. A feeling that lay halfway between satisfaction and biting disappointment washed over her.

She started to close the doors to the closet when a flutter of silk caught her eye. Toward the very back, hanging on a hook, was a flimsy, blue nightgown. Samantha seized it and looked at it carefully. It had the label of a well-known Minneapolis department store inside, announcing that the gown was petite in size.

Suddenly, a lemon zigzag of lightning flashed outside the window, illuminating the room in a ghostly light. Samantha anxiously glanced out the window. The promised violence of the storm added to her sense of uneasiness. Clutching the sheer, silken garment to her chest, she quickly spun around to leave the room. As she did, she encountered Joel.

He was standing with his hands braced against either side of the doorjamb, watching her. His dark hair fell boyishly over gold-flecked eyes that danced with mischief. To Samantha, he looked almost unbearably handsome. "That gown's almost the exact shade of your eyes, Sam," he said, his voice a whisper.

The breath left her lungs and she took a backward step. He'd startled her. The intoxicating sensuality of the room, the seeming proof of Brad's defection, Joel's pain over the loss of his friend. All of these merged in her mind, shaking her usually clear perception of a situation.

Joel crossed to her, taking the crumpled silk from her hands. His fingers played over it for a moment, then he gently placed the material next to her cheek. "Perfect," he said in a baritone that sounded as if it were backed up by a full-piece orchestra.

Samantha lifted her eyes to his and the naked desire she saw in that dark gaze mesmerized her. She stood motionless, suspended in the pounding space of her heartbeat and pulse. Joel let the nightgown slide to the floor, never taking his eyes from hers. Slowly, he inclined his head, brushing his lips lightly over her mouth, up to the tip of her nose, on to the sensitive membrane of her closed eyelids.

She felt her insides melt like butter on a warm day, her iron-clad resolve to be gone from Brad's house as quickly as possible turn to tissue paper. This was the strangest sort of arousal, not frenzied or even demanding, simply deliciously tantalizing; as tempting as trespassing in a beautiful garden. She and her husband were alone in Brad's house, uninvited, about to make love. Not very professional, one tiny, still-functioning brain cell warned her!

Joel's hand moved beneath her coat to her breast. Her mind shut off. As if in slow motion, his fingers sought and found the pouting nipple. Samantha swayed slightly in his arms. "I love you, Sam," he murmured huskily. "I've never needed you so much as I need you now. Honey, I realize I've been difficult about all of this, but I can't seem to—"

His voice drifted into the tension-charged air as his eyes fixed on the empty closet. Seizing Samantha's hand, he pulled her with him. "I've got to get out of this room," he explained quietly.

Joel led the way down the hall to the guest bedroom, which was sparsely furnished with only a bed, desk, and chair. Obviously, Brad's energies had gone into decorating the master bedroom, where he'd no doubt done most of his entertaining. But this room had a clean, unused atmosphere, establishing it as neutral territory.

Joel took a deep breath and spun Samantha around so that she was facing him. He clasped his arms around her neck, searching her wide, blue eyes with a desperate, dark gaze. "I need you—now—this minute," he said simply, burying his lips in the sweet flesh of her throat. And then lifting her up against him, he carried her to the bed. Samantha lay beneath him, reveling in the warm, hard feel of his body molded to hers. She pushed his coat to one side and reached beneath his sweater, pulling his shirt free, delighting in the tangible exploration of the rippling, muscled flesh. Joel groaned softly.

Outside, the cymbal-like clash of thunder shook the house with vibrating crescendos. The furious pelting of raindrops on the roof seemed to fall in complementary rhythms. Flashes of white-hot lightning danced by the windowpanes, their frenetic procession urged on by the turbulent motion of swirling, dark clouds.

The fury of the storm, offset by Joel's gentle caresses, was like an aphrodisiac for Samantha, who twisted restlessly to free herself of her coat. She wanted nothing more right now than to experience the feel of Joel's naked flesh, to merge their bodies with the same relentless passion that the forces of nature were displaying outside.

"Ah, Sam, you feel so good," Joel breathed. "Let me help you take this sweater off." He started to lift the cornflower blue cashmere over her head, and then his eyes fixed on a bronze object half-hidden in the recesses of the roll-top desk. He fell back down on the bed next to her, breathing hard, staring at the white expanse of ceiling.

Alarmed, Samantha bent over Joel, her chest heaving with passion, but her desires overtaken by the need to comfort him. "What is it, darling? What's wrong?"

He shook his head back and forth in disbelief. "That damned trophy! Brad and I shared it our freshman year of high school. We were co-captains of the basketball team. We went all the way to state—won, too. I let him keep it because he valued it so much. He said it was not only a symbol of achievement, but of our friendship." A bitter laugh escaped his lips. "But I guess he didn't think it was valuable enough to take along on his—his defection."

She was on the verge of trying to explain to Joel that his trust in Brad had been misplaced—all along. That trust had never been challenged before. Trust in another person was a growing entity, based on a mutual history of support—in good times as well as the bad. Joel had known Brad only in the best of situations—until now. She opened her mouth to tell Joel so, but he interrupted her.

"Damn his miserable hide!" Joel rubbed his forehead furiously, his eyes turning coal black in the dim light filtering through the bedroom windows.

"Honey," Samantha said gently, "I really do think it would be better if you let me handle this—alone. It's too hard on you, Joel. I can't stand—"

He sat up so suddenly that Samantha nearly rolled off the bed. "Are you rejecting me, too, Sam? What is it with everybody, anyway? Is this my year for abandonment, or what?"

In one agile motion, Joel rose from the bed and, tucking his shirt in with furious jabs, stalked out of the room.

Samantha scrambled from the bed, hurrying after him, stopping only to grab her coat across her arm. Then, on second thought, she rushed into the master bedroom to retrieve the nightgown. She reached the landing just as Joel's heavy tread disappeared into the rumbling thunder outside. With the shimmer of blue silk streaming behind her, Samantha rushed down the stairs.

Her heart was beating so furiously with frustration and anger, she almost forgot to lock the door. But she turned back, savagely punching the doorknob button into place and slamming the door behind her as she ran onto the porch. She took the steps to the walk two at a time, running into the midst of the storm's fury.

Lightning and thunder crashed around her as she made her way through the pouring rain to the car. Jerking the door open, she flopped onto the seat. Rivulets of water ran from her streaming hair into her eyes, her clothes dripped puddles all over the smart leather interior of the little vehicle, and her teeth were chattering from a cold that seemed to permeate the very marrow of her bones.

Joel sat silently, hunched over the steering wheel. He did not look her way. Samantha's rage was approaching the boiling point. Never, never had she been so angry with Joel.

Her chest ached with the need for release of the pent-up frustration, but it was slow in coming. In her agitated state, she had no idea how to communicate with him. The temptation was to resort to the primal scream. She stole a glance at the twitching muscle in his jaw, the throbbing pulse of his Adam's apple—and then at the trembling curve of his upper lip.

Something softened inside her, causing the red-hot ball of anger, located somewhere just beneath her rib cage, to ease a bit. *Joel was not simply angry. He was hurt*. But, she reminded herself, his hurt had lashed out at her, caught her up in its painful snare. Perhaps he really believed he was being rejected by her for reasons that had nothing to do with the case. Had he truly begun to distrust her?

The realization struck her with an uncompromising force, causing her to gasp aloud. Joel turned to face her.

"What is it?" His voice was hard, but Samantha thought she detected an edge of concern, just below the surface.

"Joel," she said carefully, "it's simply not like you to feel sorry for yourself."

He looked startled for a moment and then the heavy, black brows knit together. "That's never been part of my act, Sam, and you know it! But how would you feel if I refused to do something for you that it was in my power to do?"

The words pricked her tender vulnerability, sharp, little jabs that wounded the most sensitive part of her. That tough, flippancy—a legacy from her father—refused to surface. "Joel," she said, aware that her voice was shaking, "I would give you anything I thought was *good* for you, but I think being involved in this case is causing you—us—too much pain."

"Don't make my decisions for me, Samantha." And then he stopped. My God, he thought, I've never treated her so harshly. What's going on, anyway? I'm lashing out at all the wrong people. Self-disgust and anger filled him. Where in the hell was his compassion, the confidence in his own identity that he'd always fallen back on?

Samantha shook her head and was horrified to feel tears trickle down her face. Wiping at them furtively, she looked away from Joel. "I—I just don't want Brad to come between us! M-maybe you should—" It was hard to get the words out, but she felt she had no choice. "Maybe you should hire another detective, Joel."

Relief surged through her as he drew her swiftly into his arms. "Sam, darling, that's not what I want. I just want to feel I can trust you, depend on you. If we can't work together on this case, how are we going to face any other challenges that come our way?"

"I—I don't think that's a fair analogy, Joel," she said, sniffing against his rain-splattered shoulder. "This challenge is so personal for you."

He smoothed her hair, pressing the wet, springing tendrils down and out of her eyes. "Sam," he said softly, tilting her chin up so that her brimming, blue gaze met his, "anything we face in our marriage is bound to be personal." Gently, he added, "Don't reject me, okay? I can't take that."

The emotional roller coaster she'd been riding all day came to a screeching halt. Exhaustion crept into her cold, stiff limbs. Tiredly, she answered, "I could never reject you, Joel. But don't make me the enemy again."

He nodded, his thumbs brushing away her tears as his lips tasted their salty residue. In the fierce light of the storm, his face was darkly intense, but there was a pleading quality in his eyes. "Stay in my corner, kid," he whispered against her dewy cheek. "Please, Sam. I can't win this fight without you."

SAMANTHA SAT AT her desk, absently rubbing the furrow between her golden brows. Dr. Watson lay on the chair across from her, licking his paws and regarding his mistress with enormous green eyes that reflected his I-told-you-so attitude. "Why don't you go back to sleep?" Samantha asked her pet crossly. "I don't need you to tell me I'm in a pickle!"

Watson ignored the request and continued to fix a look of pure defiance on his out-of-sorts mistress. Burying her face in her hands, Samantha gingerly probed the lavender-tinged circles under her eyes. She hadn't slept well last night, even though Joel and she had temporarily resolved their differences. This case was growing more worrisome by the minute and, to complicate matters, the sanctity of her marriage was at stake as well.

She had tried reassuring herself with the knowledge of Joel's innate security—his conviction that a marriage worked best when each partner respected the independence of the other—and with her own memories of happier times. She remembered that only a month ago she and Joel had discussed giving an open house for Christmas, their first one as a married couple. It was a special time of year for them because they'd met the Christmas before.

Joel had claimed he would be a "long, lean Santa" for the holiday gathering. Samantha insisted she was going to eat her weight in Christmas cookies, so she could be an authentic-looking Mrs. Claus. They'd laughed

and plotted the menu together as they lay in bed one
night. And when Samantha drifted off to sleep she had
dreamed of sugar plum fairies and brightly dressed elves
for the first time since she was a child.

Now, in the cold light of today's circumstances, she
could barely recapture that party mood; in fact, she felt
more like throwing in the towel. She was tempted to
insist that Joel hire another private investigator. But she'd
suggested that once, and Joel had taken it as a personal
rejection. She couldn't afford that particular misconcep-
tion, not after the shattering episode yesterday. Besides,
she and Joel had always shared their problems, along
with their joys. That was their agreement, even if both
seemed to have forgotten it over the last few days. Solving this case satisfactorily was important to their relationship, as well as to her own feeling of pride in her
work. She needed to prove to Joel she was not only a
devoted wife, but also a dedicated professional.

Lifting her blond head with unconcealed determination, Samantha focused her attention back to her notes.
She had spent the morning at Hyperspace, interviewing
employees. When she'd finished, she'd returned to Joel's
office, struck once again by the difference between this
light, airy space and the dark, cramped quarters of the
agency. Healthy green plants flourished everywhere and
sleek, modern chrome furniture filled the room. Joel had
presented her with a cup of coffee and asked, "So, did
you find out anything more than what I'd already told
you?"

Samantha had reminded herself to ignore the slight
tone of hurt in his voice. "Not really, darling," she'd
answered smoothly. "But it's part of my job to be thor-
ough. You wouldn't send out a game cartridge without
personally checking it over, would you?"

"Not unless it was stolen before that could be accom-
plished," he'd returned bitterly.

Samantha had finished her coffee and, kissing Joel
quickly on the cheek, told him she'd be in touch later.

She had returned to the agency, made up a list of errands for Miss Davenport to run, and then gotten down to work in the privacy of her own dusty but well-loved office.

An attorney—a friend of her father's—had done her a favor by calling the major credit companies in town and using his title to elicit what information was available. Not that any of it was useful. Brad had consolidated all of his loans with a single finance company two months ago, and then paid off the amount with a check that cleared the day before he disappeared. He'd also canceled every one of his insurance policies at the same time.

Next, Samantha had spent two hours on the phone with realtors, trying to determine if Brad's house had been put on the market. But no one had it listed. Nothing.

Samantha then called the women whose names she remembered as being dates of Brad's at one time or another. Each of them denied having had any recent contact with him. Another dead end!

Running through her notes a final time, Samantha squared her shoulders and made a decision. She and Joel were going to have to fly to Minneapolis. Instinctively, Samantha felt there was something to be gained by going there, but if they didn't hurry, it might not be waiting for them. Brad's mother and former business associates might be able to shed some light on the mystery of his disappearance.

In her own mind, Samantha was convinced that Brad's eventual destination was the West Coast, locus of the video industries. But if she and Joel could stumble on something in Minneapolis that would lead them to learn Brad's exact whereabouts, it would certainly make things easier. One thing she felt confident of was that Brad would deal with the larger outfits, not bothering to mess around with the thousands of cottage industry operations that were constantly springing up, which wouldn't involve enough money.

Impatiently, Samantha fingered her tangled mass of blond curls. She had promised to call Joel. I'll have to

tell him we've got to go to Minneapolis, she thought
warily. That's going to go over well. I'm sure he's just
dying to return to the site of his boyhood allegiance with
Brad. Old memories will haunt him there . . .

The jangle of the telephone interrupted her anxious
thoughts. Watson pricked up his ears. "Do you want to
get it or shall I?" Samantha asked her nosy pet. The cat
closed one eye. "My turn, huh?"

Picking up the receiver, she said, "Lacey Detective
Agency," in her most professional voice.

"Hello yourself," a deep male voice replied. "Are you
the secretary?"

This line was an ongoing gag between them. When
they'd first met, Samantha had complained to Joel that
many male clients treated her as if she were the secretary,
instead of her father's partner.

"Nope. Secretary's gone home. I'm the cleaning lady,
mister. Nobody else's here either. They're off investigating a multimillion-dollar jewel heist in Saudi Ara-
bia."

"Aha! Pretty sharp for midafternoon! One would have
thought your blood sugar would be dropping and you'd
be dull-witted by now."

"I beg your pardon. I ate three candy bars for lunch,
so I'm fortified for the day."

"I see. You're obviously a health nut."

"An ounce of prevention's worth a pound of cure, my
janitorial friends and I always say."

"Not too original, but certainly to the point. And
speaking of cures, what do you have in mind for all this
pressure we've been living under? There must be something you can do for that!"

If he could keep things light, she would, too. "I thought
a trip might be in order. Joel, I'd like to fly to Minneapolis as soon as possible to see if we can find exact
clues as to our wayward friend's whereabouts."

There was a long pause. Samantha held her breath
and waited. Don't be upset, please, she pleaded silently.

When there was still no response, she began to chatter. "We've got to go today, if possible. Brad already has a good head start on us. But I'm a little worried about the weather. The radio says there may be a blizzard. Riding out a blizzard isn't my idea of a good time."

"No? You're a hard woman to please."

Good. He was still keeping things light. "I simply would like to live to see thirty."

"A worthy goal and one I hope I have the personal satisfaction of seeing you attain."

"Gee, thanks."

"Don't mention it. Listen, I'll be by to pick you up in an hour and we can go home and pack. Can you put your mop down long enough to call the airport and get us on an early evening flight?"

"No problem. I didn't want to do the baseboards anyway."

"See you soon, Sam." Joel's resonant voice disappeared into a metallic click.

She hung up with a sense of relief. Maybe things would be all right, after all.

"So, you really want us to drive your car to the airport?" Joel asked, barely able to keep disapproval out of his voice. He had just finished loading the large trunk of the old Pontiac with their bags, and Samantha was in the process of buckling her seat belt.

"Why not, darling? You have to admit we'll have more leg room. Joel, I love your sportscar—dearly—but it'll be such a pleasure not to arrive with lipstick on my knees. And this car's heavier than yours—"

"Okay!" Joel threw up his hands in surrender. "I give up!"

Samantha reached across to pat Joel's cheek with her gloved hand. "Even if the airport's only forty-five minutes away, I'll feel safer in a larger car. For Pete's sake, darling, we're in a storm warning!"

"Do you believe everything you hear? I thought detectives were less trusting. . . ."

Samantha shot Joel a look of pure exasperation. "Joel, I'm not relying on the weatherman's forecast alone. I happen to have two perfectly good eyes, and I can see it's snowing like crazy!"

"Hmmm . . . Two very pretty *blue* eyes, I might add."

Samantha finished adjusting her felt fedora in the car mirror and flipped the visor back. Turning to face her flatterer, she crossed her eyes. "You like 'em, huh?"

Joel ignored her demented expression. "And your hat. I like your hat. It's much better on you than that Sherlock Holmes–style hat I gave you."

She uncrossed her eyes. "Thanks. My fedora's for traveling and the other one is for cheering me up on gloomy days, sort of a whimsical reminder of who I am and what I'm about."

"I see. Perfectly clear. Well, if the hat you're wearing is for traveling, let's be off!" Joel swung the sedan away from the curb and headed in the direction of the expressway.

Four miles and an hour later, the city traffic was hopelessly snarled while the snow came down with a pure white vengeance. Blowing furiously against the frustrated motorists' windshields, the crystals trapped tires in deep, wet drifts, obscured vision, and generally created havoc for those foolish enough to try to challenge it.

"Joel," Samantha said softly, as they inched their way along behind a weaving station wagon, "I'm getting the distinct feeling we could end up spending the night in the airport—that is, if we ever reach it." She pulled her glove off and reached out to give his cheek a loving caress. Then her fingers slid inside his coat collar, massaging in tiny, circular movements before they glided back up to stroke his face again.

He let out a long whistle that ended up somewhere between a sigh and a groan. "Sam, I'm beginning to think you're not so terribly interested in our getting anywhere near a runway. In fact, I have the distinct impression you're trying to distract me from traveling any farther at all."

Samantha sighed. "Darling! What makes you think such a thing?" she asked in a voice that simulated despair. "I'm merely playing the part of a dutiful, loving wife—one who is offering you her loving strength as you battle this blizzard."

Joel chuckled, rubbing his face against her slender fingers. His dark eyes grew smoky in the subdued lighting of the car. "Yeah? Well, love, if you continue to offer me your 'loving strength,' I'm going to be sorely tempted to pull off the road and let you have your way with me."

Samantha frowned. "Hmmm . . . I can see the headline now: *Frozen Lovers Found in Old Pontiac While Blizzard Rages On . . .*"

"Might be worth it," Joel murmured, wishing he could take one hand from the wheel and caress her face. He loved her more than ever for trying to distract him from the real reason they were out in such weather. She was not only concerned about their safety, but also worried about his frame of mind, he knew. The last thought made him determined to relieve her anxieties.

Carefully negotiating an icy curve in the road, he said lightly, "Darling, I really hate to change the subject, but do you have an alternate plan for getting us to Minneapolis in a reasonable amount of time—just in case the planes have had their wings clipped?" He cocked his head and gave her a taunting look, one that was half mischief and half challenge.

"As a matter of fact, I do," she answered.

"I might have known," Joel teased. "Okay. I'm waiting with bated breath."

Samantha savored her idea for a moment and then said lightly, "Trains run in nearly anything, don't they? Let's turn around and head back into the city. We can catch a train and be in Minneapolis in eight hours—not as fast as an hour flight would get us there, but—"

"A train," Joel repeated. "I haven't been on a train in years. What a great idea!" Slowly, a grin slanted across his face. *"A really great idea!"*

"You said that already," Samantha reminded him good-naturedly.

"Yeah, I know," he replied absently. "Okay! Even if the planes are flying, we've missed our flight by now, so why not take a train? And so what if the train takes longer? It'll be safer in this storm. Right?"

Samantha regarded her husband indulgently. "Your problem-solving abilities are astounding."

Joel's mouth broke into that heart-stopping smile of his, somewhere in between little-boy wistfulness and adult-male charm. "Must be your influence. Aren't you glad you decided to work with me?"

Samantha suppressed a chuckle. He was pretty irresistible. She sighed, leaning back against the seat. "Oh, I'm a lucky, lucky woman," she answered.

The train station was crowded. People milled everywhere, dragging luggage, children, and what was left of their good humor behind them. The snow continued to fall outside, heavy swirls of white blanketing the ground. Joel and Samantha two-stepped their way through the mass of humanity, intent on reaching a ticket agent. Wedged in between a mother, father, and their three whining children, the two of them balanced their luggage perilously.

Long rows of wooden pews in the century-old building were lined with the usual assortment of winos, street people, and those who'd evidently either given up on securing a ticket or who'd been successful and were waiting to hear their train announced over the loudspeaker system.

Luggage was stacked in the aisles and Redcaps frantically scurried about, attempting to handle all of it. In direct contrast to the frantic movement of the railroad employees, Samantha and Joel found themselves in a line that seemed to be going nowhere. The large overhead clock ticked away, a constant reminder to would-be passengers that, unlike them, time did not stand still.

"At this rate," Samantha said dejectedly, "we'll be stuck here for *days*."

Joel shrugged. "We stand a better chance here than at the airport, Sam."

She looked at him. "You're probably right."

"Now, don't worry, love," Joel chided. "We'll get a train."

Thirty minutes later, they were actually able to see a counter directly in front of them, where disorderly crowds were gathered. Another quarter of an hour passed and they finally found themselves facing a man whose composure had long since left him. He made a feeble attempt to force his mouth into a smile, but it failed and came out looking like a grimace instead.

Patiently, Joel managed to charm him into exhausted acquiescence, and twenty minutes later, clutching their tickets, they boarded the train to Minneapolis. Moments later they collapsed into their seats.

"Success," Samantha sighed wearily.

"Victory," Joel agreed tiredly.

They sat quietly for a few minutes, watching the hustle and bustle of the passengers with detached interest. Joel rested his hand lightly on Samantha's arm. She leaned back, sighing. Even through the heavy wool of her sweater, she was aware of those disturbing quivers of desire that assailed her every time he touched her. How was it that she was still as in love with her husband as she had been on the day he proposed?

Snuggling closer to him, Samantha closed her eyes and made a fervent wish: *Please don't ever let this change between us*. She never wanted to end up as some married couples did, constantly quarreling and bickering; or worse, totally oblivious to the other's presence. Either situation would be intolerable. She'd been so fortunate to meet and marry Joel. He was, in spite of his human imperfections, the person with whom she wanted to share the rest of her life.

Her mind snapped back to reality as the conductor shouted his final "All aboard!" and the train creaked out of the station. Joel seemed revived once they were moving. "Isn't this great, Sam? Just like the good old days. A shot of nostalgia."

His enthusiasm was contagious and Samantha straightened to look out the window. The train was gathering speed, whizzing past the last of the metropolitan landmarks and on through the white countryside. Somehow the whole nightmarish adventure began to take on the tones of a romantic escapade. Sitting next to Joel, she felt reassured, protected from nature's elements by a massive iron engine that, no doubt, had steamed its way through many storms before, steadily, fearlessly pounding its way over the tracks to its appointed destinations.

Samantha glanced over at Joel. His profile was eagerly set, his dark hair, still damp from the snow, glistening as it fell carelessly onto his forehead. He had the look of a man who was totally enthralled with his life and perfectly capable of handling any situation that might arise—except the shattering devastation of Brad's guilt, or his wife's part in proving it. For the first time in her life she realized clearly she might be in a no-win situation.

Shuddering, Samantha clutched her cardigan. There was so much at stake in this case!

Joel squeezed her hand. "Hey, legs, how about a little drink in the club car? We can warm our hands and hearts with some good whiskey."

"That's the best idea you've had all day, darling. Lead on."

She clung to Joel's arm as they lurched their way through the rocking cars. She felt safe, proper somehow with her arm linked through her husband's. Oh, what a good-looking, sexy guy he was. Sometimes she couldn't believe how lucky she was. Even when the going was rough...

Joel gave her arm an affectionate squeeze, as if he were sharing her thoughts. He steered her into the club car, and they gratefully sank into two chairs at the last unoccupied table. A waiter in an impeccably white coat took their order and within minutes placed it in front of them. Samantha sipped at her whiskey, enjoying the warm relaxation the amber liquid induced, allowing the tension to leave her neck and shoulders.

"Just what the doctor ordered?" Joel said.

Samantha nodded. "But one's my limit. As Dad always said, the image of the private investigator as a hard drinker is a lot of malarkey. Liquor slows down your reflexes and your deductive reasoning..."

"Sam," Joel began slowly, "I'm a little concerned about something. In fact, it's bothered me a lot lately. The thought of your being in real danger makes my blood run cold. And full-line investigation can certainly be dangerous!"

The muscles in her neck began to knot again. "Women detectives have their own modes of defense, Joel—often more subtle than those men use, but, nevertheless, quite effective. Sometimes in a tight situation, you have to depend on your verbal expertise or slight deceptions... Whatever it takes."

"You've never been entirely on your own in a dangerous situation," Joel said firmly. "Your father was always there with you."

"Are you questioning my competence, Joel?"

Dark eyes captured her intensely blue gaze. "Don't twist my words around, Sam. Doesn't a husband have every right to be concerned for his wife's safety—and vice versa, for that matter?"

She forced her mind to make a logical analysis of his comments. His usual enthusiastic belief in people seemed to have been eroded by Brad's defection. Not only that, but hadn't his trust in her slipped somewhat since the theft of Catwalk? Damn Brad Davies anyway! He'd turned their lives inside out. Before this whole incident, Joel would have allowed her to sidestep a drunken neighbor's advances, would have trusted her to handle it. She still vividly remembered the scene at their party with Joel literally shoving the man out the door...

Wait a minute! The little voice inside Samantha's head was trying to tell her something. Joel hadn't known for certain that Brad was the thief until the next day—or had he? Had he really known, deep down, all along that Brad was the most logical suspect, that Mary Beth—

Her thoughts were cut off by the metallic grating of wheels. A whistle shrieked in the darkness as the train began to lurch unsteadily, attempting to ease its way to a stop. Suddenly, the lumbering vehicle came to a crashing halt, spilling their drinks into their laps. Samantha was nearly thrown from her seat. Screams echoed throughout the club car. Joel leaned forward across the table to seize her hand and pull her upright. Then he stood, gathering her to the warm protection of his chest. "Are you all right, Sam?" he asked anxiously.

"I'm fine," she murmured, trying to express more resolve than she felt. Around her, the shrieks of other passengers were just dying down. "What's happened?"

He shook his head. "I don't know for sure. Let's see if anyone else needs a hand."

No one was seriously injured, though many appeared badly shaken. Samantha and Joel were able to be of help to some of the others in the club car, helping them get to their feet and retrieve their scattered belongings. One woman appeared to be on the verge of hysteria and Samantha put an arm around her, soothing her with a gentle touch and calming words. "Everything's going to be fine," she assured the woman.

A porter entered the car, followed by a white-faced conductor. "The train won't be moving again for several hours," the conductor announced. "We've got huge drifts blocking the tracks. This is one of the worst blizzards we've had in years." All that could be done, he went on to explain, was to wait out the worst of the storm. Then, in the morning, perhaps the train could be shoveled out and they would continue. Joel whispered urgently to the conductor for a few minutes. The uniformed man slowly shook his head before he turned to leave.

So much for thinking of this train trip as a romantic adventure, Samantha thought. Stranded! In a blizzard yet! Wonderful! In old movies, things like this had seemed exciting, but then she had been merely a spectator, munching away happily on popcorn in the safety of the neighborhood theater. Heck, she told herself, in movies the Royal Mounties would come to the aid of the beleaguered hero and heroine—or some other equally miraculous way out would be found. But what were *they* going to do?

Joel put his arm around her. "Come on, kid, I've got just the thing for you," he drawled in a mediocre imitation of Humphrey Bogart.

Samantha forced herself to smile. "I think the line is, 'Here's looking at you, kid,'" she corrected.

"Whatever." Joel gave an elegant shrug. "Follow me, okay? Trust me on this one."

Obediently, Samantha followed Joel through the maze of cars. Many people were already trying to find comfortable positions in which to sleep in their cramped seats. Porters rushed by, carrying trays of sandwiches and pots of steaming coffee. A general calm descended. Some passengers were even laughing and joking among themselves. It was as if everyone had accepted the situation and was determined to make the best of it.

They were almost to the back of the train when Joel turned to her and put his hands on her shoulders. "No thanks necessary, Sam. A simple kiss will suffice."

She looked at him suspiciously. "What's up, doc? Do you have a limo waiting outside with its engine running?"

"Nothing quite that good, darling, but close. If we have to spend the entire night on this train, I've decided we should do it in style. This isn't the Orient Express, but a berth in which to sleep is better than squeezing our long legs into regular seats, don't you think?"

Samantha's enormous eyes registered delighted surprise and her mouth dropped open as Joel led her into a double roomette. Samantha stared at the bunk beds. "How in the world did you manage to pull this off?" she asked incredulously.

Joel looked smug. "I think the appropriate term is *bribery,* my dear. I paid my bucks and got one of the last roomettes available on this iron horse."

"You're a man of resource indeed, darling," Samantha said, placing her hands on either side of Joel's face and drawing his mouth to hers. Their lips met in a long, lingering kiss; as they pulled slowly apart, she traced the dimpled concave of his chin. "You and Cary Grant," she murmured.

"He's eighty and I'm not," Joel teasingly reminded her. "Better watch out!"

"I'm ready for anything, big boy," Samantha bragged.

"Well, don't change your mind, love. A porter should be here soon with some dinner, a nice bottle of wine, and clean sheets. After all that's taken care of, we can have dessert." Joel trailed his fingers down her cheekbone, along the smooth skin of her throat, to the pounding pulse at its base.

"You know, darling," Samantha whispered, "I'd be just as happy to skip the entree. Desserts are my favorite part—"

A knock on the door interrupted her suggestion. Joel gave her a wry look and let the porter in. Immediately the man spread the small table by the window with a cloth and steaming, covered dishes. Then he turned his attention to putting clean bedding on each berth. Satisfied that he'd completed his requested tasks, he exited with a polite nod.

Samantha sat down across from Joel and lifted the cover from her plate to survey the food. Tantalizing aromas wafted through the roomette. "Have I told you lately that I love you?" she asked gratefully.

Joel gave her a look of mocking dismay. "Sam! Is that as original as you're going to get?"

Turquoise eyes shone with promise. "Honey, you ain't seen nothin' yet," she drawled, Mae West fashion.

"Oh, I hope not," Joel returned. "Now eat before your food gets cold, Sam, and then we'll see if you're all you claim to be!"

Half an hour later, Samantha leaned back in her chair and groaned. "Oh, I'm stuffed! I guess I was hungrier than I thought!"

"The food was actually quite delicious," Joel agreed. "How about a little glass of Amaretto to top things off?"

She shook her head. "No, thanks, darling, I couldn't do that to my poor stomach."

Joel poured himself a glass of the almond-flavored after-dinner drink and took her hand, gently caressing each finger.

Outside the snow continued to blow and swirl, forming white funnels against the black backdrop of starless sky, punctuated here and there by a blinking light on a tower. The sound of the wind cut an eerie whistle in the darkness. Samantha snuggled back into her seat, finding that she was enjoying the situation for the first time. The roomette was toasty and warm.

Joel, taking a long sip of his drink, allowed his eyes the pleasure of wandering over his wife's face. She seemed to have relaxed completely. Her thickly lashed eyes were halfway closed and her full, kissable lips were parted slightly. Blond tendrils of hair framed the creamy skin of her flushed face. She looked so vulnerable that he felt a rushing urge to cradle her in his arms, to protect her from the strom, from anything or anyone who might harm her.

He wondered idly if she was anything like her mother. He'd seen photographs of the woman who had died when

Samantha was very young. The two women looked alike, but there were no real indications of the mother's personality in Samantha. What kind of person had she been? How had she withstood the rigors of her husband's job with its odd hours, long absences, and constant exposure to potential danger?

"Sam, are you going to sleep on me?"

"Nope. I was watching you watch me. What were you thinking just now?"

He released her hand and tilted the glass to his lips, finishing the last of the Amaretto. "I was wondering if you remember anything about your mother—what she was like, how she reacted to your father's job. She must have been worried a great deal of the time."

Samantha stiffened. Was this Joel's subtle way of telling her that being married to a detective put an undue strain on a relationship? "I don't remember much about her," she said slowly. "But Dad often said how much he looked forward to coming home to her, after a long day. He missed her until the day he died."

"I wonder if he ever guessed how hard it must have been for her to support him in his work," Joel mused.

"She knew what he did for a living when she agreed to marry him," Samantha retorted curtly. "His work was part of him, another commitment that in no way lessened his desire for family life. I'm sure she understood that."

"But you don't know for sure, do you, Samantha?" Joel persisted.

She rose from the table. "I'm exhausted. I'm going to bed," she stated flatly, grabbing her smaller suitcase and awkwardly lugging it toward the berths. "Do you want the top or lower?" she asked.

"Lower," he answered impassively.

"Fine. Good night." Samantha climbed the ladder and hurled herself into the narrow bed. Joel snapped the light off and she heard the water splash into the room's small, stainless steel basin. She smiled, a little ironically. Joel's fastidiousness was one of the things she often teased him about. He rarely entered a room that had a sink without washing his hands.

And why didn't *I* think to wash up? she wondered. Too busy cutting off my nose to spite my face, I suppose. Well, she'd be damned if she'd climb back down to prepare properly for bed. It might give Joel too much satisfaction.

She lay in total darkness, trying to wrestle her way out of her sweater. The space was small and she bumped her head twice. Once she had the sweater off, she decided to tackle her slacks. Slowly, she inched her way out of the finely woven wool, scraping her elbow on the edge of the bed in the process. Swell! I may bleed to death on top of everything else, she thought despairingly.

She had just made up her mind to climb back down, turn on the light, and finish undressing when she heard Joel climbing into the lower berth. That made up her mind. With renewed determination, she contorted her body until she was able to wiggle out of her bra, then her panties.

It took her some minutes of clever maneuvering to get into her nightgown, which she finally located by the feel of its flannel softness. She jammed the suitcase into the lower corner of the bed and curled up into a ball. For half an hour she lay there, trying to relax. But it was impossible. The tight quarters had forced her muscles into hard knots. Worse, her body kept sending her messages in response to Joel's nearness. She alternated between anger and desire as she listened to his even breathing. How could he sleep with such tension between them?

Exasperated, lonely, and cold, she rolled over and gingerly extended one leg over the side of the berth in an attempt to stretch out. A stabbing pain assailed the calf of her leg. "Ouch! Oh, damn!"

"Samantha? What is it?" Joel jumped from his bed and hit the light switch.

She tried to sit up so that she could assure him she was okay, that he could turn the light out, that she was sorry she'd awakened him—but she couldn't. The pain moved all the way up her calf to her thigh, immobilizing her with its intensity.

Joel was by her side instantly and before she could protest, he'd gathered her into his arms and gently lowered her to the floor. "What is it? A charley horse?" he asked kindly, bending over her. She nodded, unable to speak. "Okay. I'll have that fixed in a few minutes. Try to lie still."

He grasped the calf of her leg and began to knead it, working the magic of his fingertips into the relentless knot of muscle. Samantha bit her lip. Slowly, she felt the circulation return to her aching limb. Joel continued to work his way up her leg, massaging and caressing it carefully, the warmth of his hands comforting and soothing. Samantha lay with her eyes closed, giving herself over completely to his gentle ministrations. She was barely aware of herself or him, only of the pain leaving her body. Then she came to with a start. Joel's hand was on her thigh, massaging it with a sensual pleasure that brought a gasp to her lips.

"This is some muscle cramp," he said softly. "Goes all the way up your leg."

"Uh, yeah. It does—did—" she hastily corrected herself. She started to sit up, but her nose bumped Joel's bare chest, and then her eyes fixed on the thin fabric of his pajama bottoms that rode low on his lean hips.

A firm hand pushed her back down. "Easy, Sam. The doctor's not done. Just lie back and relax. What's the matter with you, anyway? Afraid I'll find a concealed weapon?"

She wanted to be indignant, intended to raise herself up on her elbows and tell him to stop, that she was fine. But she did none of those things. Instead she broke into laughter—glorious, uninhibited peals. Joel had achieved what she'd been unable to do by herself—released her

tensions with his concern, then his humor. Both charmed
her.

He moved his hand from her thigh and lowered himself onto her heaving chest. "Aha! Patient's obviously
hysterical. I have just the remedy for that."

He cut off her laughter with his lips, moving them
deliberately, slowly pressing his tongue into the warm
recesses of her mouth, teasing and taunting her with the
hint of indescribable pleasure. His hand moved to the
back of her neck, through the golden mass of hair to
the top of her spine, sending fiery pinpoints of arousal
through her. Her arms came up and encircled his neck,
her fingers catching and weaving their way through the
thick, dark hair. Joel withdrew his lips from hers and
looked into her face, his eyes drinking in the shape and
texture of each lovely plane. "I want you, Samantha,"
he said simply, only the huskiness of his voice belying
his urgency.

"Me, too," she said.

Joel got up and stripped the beds, throwing off the
blankets and sheets, arranging them in a bed of sorts on
the floor. Then he switched off the light and turned on
a small night light inside the compartment. Samantha
hadn't noticed it before. Its muted glow cast shadows on
his sinewy frame and filled the room with soft radiance,
heightened by the white, drifting flakes that fell outside
the window. He bent over and carefully lifted her onto
the nest of bedclothes.

Samantha's blue gaze fastened on the rippling curve
of Joel's shoulder muscle, the taut, strong cords vibrating
in his neck. "I love you very much," she said softly.

"I love you, too, Sam...enough that I'm going to
try to overlook what you're wearing," he answered mischievously.

She looked down at her chest and groaned. She'd
packed the wrong nightgown! Instead of the flowered
flannel with its seductively low neckline and lace trim,

she'd brought her Garfield the cat nightshirt, purchased once as a gag. The joke had been effective, but once was enough. "Oh, dear," she cried. "I knew I should have taken more time to pack!"

Joel chuckled, running his fingers lingeringly over Garfield's whiskers. "Don't get me wrong, Sam. I'd make love to you if you were wearing Army fatigues, but having Garfield's picture right here on your chest makes me nervous. It reminds me of Dr. Watson—ready to pounce!" He withdrew his hand from her chest, letting one finger graze the swollen bud of her breast.

He lifted the gown over her head in one lazy motion, gathering her to him by placing the breadth of his hand under the small of her back. He covered the top of her head with kisses, then moved on down to her eyes, forcing the lids closed as he skimmed them with his lips. Then his mouth brushed past her nose, her throat, the sensitive spot on her shoulder. The pressure of his hand on her back increased slightly and she found herself hoping his mouth would find the aching tips of her breasts.

Almost as if he'd heard her unspoken plea, Joel kissed the rounded flesh, quickly seeking each nipple, wetting and warming it with his probing tongue. Fingertips delightfully encircled both buds, kneading them with exquisite tenderness, until they rose to meet his cupped palms. "You are so lovely, Samantha," he breathed.

Lovemaking was always good between them, but this time Joel knew it would be ecstasy—something to remember always. He wanted Samantha as he'd never wanted her before. Driven by the force of a possession he could not fully understand, he wanted to consume her rose-scented body, fold her inside him, brand her flesh with searing kisses.

As he entered her moist center, he felt total release for the first time in days, liberated from his own sense of caution, his terrible disbelief and anger, none of which really had anything to do with Samantha, yet had managed somehow to tarnish their relationship. She was all softness, warmth, and rapture. She was completely his.

A small corner of Samanatha's brain that remained open to rational thought nudged her as she and Joel experienced each other's bodies, reminding her to savor the moment, to remember it. She might need the strength of the memory to reassure her in the struggle to return to where they'd been before Brad's defection. And then she forgot to concentrate on anything other than the blinding, pulsing desire exploding inside her. Totally absorbed in the hot light of passion, she wrapped her arms more tightly around Joel's taut hips, and began the delightful journey into love's secret, safe place.

Colors caught fire in a blend of sound, sight, and motion. They whirled and spun behind her eyes, dancing and beckoning her to come just a little farther—on over the rainbow, flying as high as she could, beyond the rim of the earth...

They lay, damp bodies glistening, protected from the chill of the room by the warmth of their sustained passion. White, downy flakes drifted on the wind outside, but they were not falling with the gusto of a blizzard any longer, simply swaying to the slow, sensuous rhythms of a lovers' waltz.

— 8 —

SAMANTHA HAD NEVER been to Minneapolis before, but it certainly was living up to its cold-weather reputation. The rental car's radio announced that the wind-chill factor made it twenty degrees below zero and that, over the last week, another foot of snow had fallen, bringing the total ground accumulation to a little under two feet.

The largest city in Minnesota was on the Mississippi River which, according to the radio, was clogged with ice floes that detained barges just as the drifting snow had held up the train until they had been shoveled out at five the next morning. Traffic lumbered heavily through the main arteries of the city, already cleaned by plows, and as Joel skillfully maneuvered the front-wheel-drive car, Samantha marveled at the beautiful aftermath of the blizzard. Now that the storm was over and the sun had come out, it was hard to believe that this spectacular, prismatic scene could have ever seemed threatening.

"It's beautiful, Joel," she breathed. "Like a winter wonderland."

"Yes, I know," he remarked absently. More thoughtfully, he added, "But it's deceiving, Sam. We're far enough north that the temperatures drop quickly, and the drop alone can kill those who aren't prepared for it. The elderly, especially. This beauty has to be considered a dangerous attraction."

Samantha's appreciation of the winter loveliness of the city faded as she pondered Joel's comments. *A dangerous attraction.* Was he talking only of the weather?

For him, this city held memories, some of which were more deeply buried than the snow-laden ground. She shivered involuntarily, moving closer to Joel.

"Read me that address again, Sam," he said.

She complied with his request, referring to her notepad, its cover labeled simply "Brad." Within minutes they were in a parking garage next to a multistoried building. An attendant directed them to an interior elevator and Samantha and Joel made a dash for it, huddling together for warmth. Running her finger along the printed directory, Samantha located Addison Advertising Agency. She punched the button for the eighth floor and squeezed Joel's hand reassuringly as the elevator glided smoothly upward.

There must be a lead here, she thought desperately. Her legwork the other day had yielded very little of consequence. The blue negligee was one of the few possible clues. The brand label had been of no help, though the size indicated the gown was for a small woman, probably under five feet five.

Samantha was convinced Brad's motivation for stealing Catwalk must be monetary gain, but she felt there might be underlying circumstances as well—perhaps deeply rooted psychological ones. Could a woman playing on Brad's weakness for feminine charms have been the catalyst for this crime?

She had never been able to confide in her husband her essential feelings about his oldest friend, had never complained about the sly innuendos Brad directed her way. Brad was an attractive man, and she'd always been sure he would get what he wanted in life—no matter the cost. But if one were concerned about her husband's happiness and peace of mind, she did not divulge such information. After all, Samantha had no real proof of anything and Brad's glib, slick style was his protective charm.

Before Brad stole Catwalk, she'd never thought of him as dangerous. She saw him as simply a little fast-paced for her taste. But now she realized he was much more than a mover and a shaker. The other side of his smooth, gregarious personality was darker than she'd ever imagined.

The elevator came to a halt on the eighth floor and Samantha turned to Joel. It was time to play the parts indicated by the outfits they'd donned shortly before leaving the train. "Got your lines down?" she asked breezily, already falling into the role she'd assigned herself.

Joel's mouth broke into a generous smile. His killer smile, so much like Brad's. Dark eyes caught and held her bright blue ones. "Perfectly. We rehearsed so much on that snow-bound train that I'm sure I could say them in my sleep. But you've forgotten something, haven't you?"

"What?" she asked innocently.

"Your gum," he reminded her.

"Oops! Thanks, partner." Samantha reached into her purse and extracted a piece of bubble gum. Popping it into her mouth, she chewed frantically for a few seconds and then blew an experimental bubble. "What d'ya think?" she asked, running her words together.

Joel chuckled. "You're a woman of hidden vices, Sam. And to think that all this time I thought I was married to a lady. Where did you pick up such nasty habits?"

She wrinkled her nose. Taking a deep breath, she said, "Okay, darling. Let's hope someone at the agency falls for our 'just plain folks' act enough to give us some information about Brad."

"I hope you're right, Sam. God knows we can't afford to make mistakes at this point. Time is running out . . . But the agency *is* the most logical place to start," he reassured her quickly.

"I can't guarantee anything, darling," Samantha said apologetically. "In this business, you have to rely on hunches—and that's all we've got right now."

Joel nodded. "I understand. Okay, let's get this over

with." He loped jerkily down the hall in a perfect imitation of a cowboy who's been in the saddle too long. Samantha clung to his arm, popping her gum and undulating her hips. They gyrated through the door of the agency and greeted the startled receptionist.

"Hi, there!" Joel drawled. "Wonder if you could give us a little of your precious time?"

The mousy young woman blinked as she took in Joel's accent, his tightly cut jeans and the open neck of the plaid shirt that rested casually against the collar of his unbuttoned sheepskin coat. She started to open her mouth and then closed it. Joel took full advantage of her hesitance. He smiled. She melted.

"What do you have in mind?" the woman asked a little breathlessly, removing her glasses in an obvious effort to improve the impression she would make.

"Somethin' I'm sure you can handle, honey. This is my sister, Rosie." Joel jerked a thumb at Samantha, who popped her gum as she extended her hand.

"Pleased to meetcha," "Rosie" gushed. "I'm kind of a fright, I guess. Me and Lou here's been on a bus for three days. Then that damned blizzard come up and we had to switch to a train. But," she added, smoothing the front of her tight magenta sweater and angling a lean, jean-clad hip onto the receptionist's desk, "the important thing is, we made it!"

"Yes, well," the brown-haired woman replied, "Yes, you did. Certainly. Ah... well, how might I be of assistance to you? You... you didn't," she said hesitantly, "come all this way to sing a jingle did you?"

Joel leaned closer to the woman, letting her have the full effect of his opened shirt. "A jingle?"

"Uh, yes. Sometimes we get hopefuls who think they have ideas—" The receptionist took a deep breath as Joel bent even nearer. "Ideas for ads," she finished uncertainly.

Joel laughed; a deep, resonant chuckle. "No, ma'am. Me and Rosie are looking for a friend. Actually, we met him a few months ago. He was kinda sweet on sis here, and since we're in town to close a little land deal, we thought we'd surprise him and drop by."

"Oh. I see," the receptionist answered, but it was plain she didn't.

"Name's Brad Davies," Samantha said, running her fingers over the brown leaves of an unhealthy plant on the desk. "This needs watering, y'know?"

The woman ignored her and turned her attention back to Joel. "I really wish I could help you—uh—Lou. But Mr. Davies hasn't been with Addison for some time."

"Well, what d'ya know? That's a darned shame," Joel roared. "And we were so anxious to see him again. Rosie, in particular."

Samantha blew a bubble, then deftly recaptured the transparent pink globe between her teeth. "You got a forwardin'?"

"No, I'm sorry I don't," the receptionist apologized, her eyes resting appreciatively on Joel as he stretched languidly, shoving his Stetson hat back on his glossy, dark hair. "But maybe I can find someone who does. Wait here and I'll go ask."

She sailed hurriedly into an inner office and Samantha and Joel exchanged conspiratorial looks. Within a few minutes, the receptionist returned with a red-haired woman in tow. "This is Miss Gable, Mr. Davies's former secretary," she explained. "Mr. Addison and his partner are out of town today, but perhaps Miss Gable can help you."

"What is it exactly that you want?" the secretary asked curtly, directing the question to Samantha.

"Honey, I just wanted to look Brad up and say 'hi' for old-times' sake."

The petite, busty redhead's large green eyes widened and then narrowed. "I see." A well-manicured hand touched the diamond studs in her ears as she looked Samantha up and down. "I'm afraid I can't be of any help to you. When Brad—Mr. Davies—left the firm, he didn't disclose his future plans."

"Oh," Samantha said wistfully. "Some shame! We had a lotta fun down in Oklahoma awhile back. He said he was there on business—in Tulsa—and we struck up a real good relationship." She popped her gum for emphasis.

The well-endowed secretary bit her lip, fumbling with a row of tiny buttons on her silk blouse. "I see. Well, Mr. Davies's personal life is—was—a mystery to me. I certainly can't give you any information," she finished icily.

Joel sighed and threw an arm around Samantha. "Well, listen, you've been real nice. Both of you," he added, smiling at the receptionist. "I'm sorry we took up your valuable time. Guess we'll just have to finish our business in town and go back home. Maybe Brad'll contact Rosie here one of these days."

"Yeah," Samantha drawled. "Bet he will. We had too good a thing goin' for him not to."

Miss Gable leveled a scorching look on Samantha. Then, turning on a skyscraper heel, she marched back into the interior offices.

"Sorry," the receptionist said in a tone that implied she regretted more than just Brad Davies's absence. Her liquid gaze rested on Joel. "Miss Gable seemed so interested in talking to you; I thought perhaps she could be helpful."

"Hey! That's all right, honey! You just keep warm, hear? Maybe I'll be back to see you sometime." Joel seized Samantha's arm and steered her quickly out of the agency's waiting room.

Once in the hall, they made a beeline for the elevator. "You were pretty good in there, cowboy," Samantha said admiringly, extracting the pink wad of gum from her mouth and depositing it in a waste receptacle.

Joel removed the Stetson. "Thanks, partner. Whew! The hatband on this damned thing gave me a headache!"

"The price one pays, I'm afraid, for illusion," Samantha retorted mischievously. "But don't think of yourself as the Lone Ranger, pal. If I don't get out of these jeans, I'll never walk right again!"

Joel drew her into his arms, reaching over her shoulder to punch the elevator button. "Too bad we didn't learn anything, though," he whispered in her ear.

Samantha gratefully rested in his warm embrace. "Yeah," she remarked absently. Then she exclaimed excitedly, "Joel! Brad's secretary!"

"Seemed a little flustered, didn't she?" Joel murmured, resting his lips against Samantha's honey-scented hair. "Think that means anything in particular—more, that is, than probably being a left-behind lover of Brad's?"

"Maybe," Samantha answered. "Her behavior was telling. But her *height* is important, too."

Joel stepped back and tipped her chin up, his dark eyes looking curiously into her face. "Sam, what in the hell are you talking about?"

She reached out to trace the dimpled cleft of his chin. "Miss Gable is under five feet five, darling. I could tell, in spite of those high heels. And her—uh—bosom probably looks pretty spectacular in a size petite blue silk negligee. Follow me?"

Joel regarded her quizzically for a moment and then, arching a heavy, black brow, he hooked his thumbs in his belt, adopting the laid-back swagger of a true Westerner. "Darlin', there's no moss growing on your back, that's for sure!"

Fifteen minutes after leaving the Addison Advertising Agency, Samantha and Joel pulled into a service station and split up to change out of their Western clothes. Dressed in more comfortable attire, they met back at the car. Samantha had chosen a teal wool blazer with matching straight skirt; Joel wore a Harris tweed sports coat and gray flannel slacks.

"I figure," Samantha said, breathless from the cold, "that we should pay a visit to Brad's mother now. We've got the time. Miss Gable shouldn't get off until five o'clock, according to the office hours that were posted on the agency's door. We'll have plenty of time to get back downtown to follow her when she leaves work."

Joel opened the car door and helped Samantha inside with her overnight bag. Then he handed her his carryall to toss onto the back seat. Hurrying around the front of the vehicle, he slid his long, lean frame behind the steering wheel. "I wonder if I should call her first," he muttered, more to himself than to Samantha.

"Whatever you think, darling," Samantha responded lightly. This visit was bound to be painful for Joel, and she wanted him to do whatever would make him the most comfortable.

"Be right back, Sam," he said abruptly.

She watched him through the glass front of the service station. His dark head was bent in concentration as he looked up Mrs. Davies's number in the directory. He bit off a leather glove, letting it dangle between his teeth while he dialed. Then Samantha saw him quickly shove the glove in his coat pocket and speak into the receiver. Slowly, a smile broke across his face, and he looked through the window, making a "V" for victory sign. Samantha smiled back, blowing him a kiss.

They made the trip to Mrs. Davies's house in relative silence, winding through affluent suburbs until they came to a section of Minneapolis that featured rows of small, plain homes. They all looked so much alike, one seemed indistinguishable from the other. But Joel swung the car with surety into a hilly driveway.

Mrs. Davies's house was the same putty color as the other dwellings on the block, but it sported a brightly painted window box and a neatly trimmed hedge. An obvious effort to improve mediocre surroundings, Samantha thought methodically, as the door swung open before Joel could raise his hand to knock. A faded, female version of Brad enveloped him warmly in her arms.

"Joel! It's been so long—I just can't believe it!" the woman exclaimed. Releasing him reluctantly, she turned toward Samantha. "And you're his wife, Samantha, of course! I might have known that this handsome devil would catch someone pretty as you!" Mrs. Davies reached out to hug Samantha and then drew back quickly. "Lord! I don't know what's the matter with me—it's freezing out here! Come on inside, please!"

Samantha and Joel followed Brad's mother into a small living room. Every piece of furniture had seen better days and the carpet was worn and frayed, but there was a spotless, cozy appeal to the shabby room.

Mrs. Davies took their coats and ushered them to a slightly sagging horsehair sofa. "Sit down, please. I'll be right back. Oh, there's so much to catch up on, Joel!"

As soon as Mrs. Davies left the room, Samantha turned to Joel. "Somehow I imagined Brad's background as more affluent than this, darling. You could eat off the floor of this little place, but it isn't the upper-middle-class house I expected."

"They've never had much, Sam," Joel answered. "You see, Brad's father died when he was still in grade school. Mrs. Davies worked hard to give Brad everything she could. He's the pride of her life."

Sadness crept over Samantha, but it was quickly replaced by anger. Brad's mother had sacrificed so much for him. Why hadn't he helped her more financially, after he'd gone out on his own? Addison Advertising was a big firm and Brad had been a top executive. He must have earned a substantial salary—and she knew he'd been making good money at Hyperspace.

Mrs. Davies came back into the room, her cheeks flushed with the pleasure of having company. "Here we go. Some of those homemade sugar cookies you always loved as a child, Joel, and hot tea to go with them." Mrs. Davies set the tray of refreshments down on a battered, pine coffee table in front of the sofa and eased herself into a chair across from Samantha and Joel. Looking fondly at the couple as she poured each of them a steaming cup of tea, she said sadly, "I was so sorry to hear Brad was leaving your firm, Joel. When he called to tell me, I tried to talk him out of it, but you know how headstrong he's always been." She laughed indulgently as if to excuse her criticism of her son.

Joel shifted uncomfortably. "Yes. I hated to see him go, too. But I suppose he wanted to move on to bigger opportunities."

Mrs. Davies sighed. "He tells me he thinks he's got a wonderful job sewn up out in California." She chuckled. "Said after growing up in Minneapolis, he was ready to live somewhere warm."

Samantha thought quickly. "So, Brad's settled in California now?"

The older woman rubbed her brow. "Oh, honey, I don't know if Brad's ever *settled* anywhere. But he's out there. I don't even know exactly where. He said he'd call me again as soon as this new job took hold. Seems it's unclear whether he'll have to travel a lot with this company or work in an office in Los Angeles—"

"I've forgotten the name of the firm," Joel interjected.

Mrs. Davies frowned. "I don't think he ever mentioned the name, Joel. He just said it was an import-export business." She smoothed the front of her cotton housedress and then spoke cheerfully, "Anyway, I'm so glad to see you two! Imagine you here on business, and being thoughtful enough to interrupt your busy schedule to visit me!"

"I've never forgotten the hours I spent here with you and Brad," Joel said kindly. "You were like a second mother to me. I wouldn't dream of being in town and not stopping by."

Mrs. Davies's wrinkled face crinkled into an expression of genuine warmth. "I always enjoyed having you around." She paused, her cloudy blue eyes reflecting deeply felt emotion. "You know, Brad has always been a joy to me. He's so handsome and talented, but I felt a father might have made a big difference in his life, given him a little more direction. That's why I was so happy he was able to spend so much time with you and your parents. I hoped some of the military values would rub off on Brad. I tried, of course, to teach him things like dedication and perseverance—but I had to earn a living, and there never seemed to be enough time to spend with him. Brad's a wonderful son, but I do worry sometimes about his lack of stick-to-itiveness."

The old woman chuckled. "Honestly, Samantha, the only way I ever got all of my windows washed was if Joel came over to help. I'm afraid my son was inclined to do two or three windows and then wander off. But if Joel was here, Brad and he would make a race out of the whole thing..."

"Oh, but that's typical of boys, Mrs. Davies," Samantha said graciously. "I'm sure that as an adult Brad is loyal to whatever his goals are."

"Thank you, dear. It's hard growing up without a father—especially if one is a boy." The tall, thin woman brushed a straying strand of gray-blond hair off her forehead. "After Brad's father deserted us, things were really very difficult..."

Deserted them? Brad told Joel his father had died; Joel had spoken of this often. Samantha turned to look at her husband, almost afraid to see how this latest news was affecting him. Joel's face was drawn. One more lie, his expression said. Silently, Samantha returned his gaze.

"I do hope Brad's new woman friend is nice, like you, Samantha," Mrs. Davies said wistfully, picking up the threads of the conversation. "If he could just find a good woman and get his life in order, stop flitting from place to place..."

"Oh, my!" Samantha exclaimed. "He never breathed a word about a serious relationship. He's been holding out on us."

Mrs. Davies made a clucking sound with her tongue. "Well, I hope he's telling the truth and not just placating an old woman who's made no secret of wanting grandchildren. I'd really like a daughter-in-law—and when

Brad called me, he mentioned that he was seeing someone seriously. I think she's supposed to join him in California . . . The odd thing is I got the feeling he knew this woman before he came to work with you, Joel. Now why did I think that? Hmmm. This old brain isn't as sharp as it used to be!"

"Well, it's hard to keep these things straight, Mrs. Davies. We all have so much going on in our own lives . . ." Samantha smiled.

The older woman shook her head. "No, I really don't. I'm afraid I'm just getting old and forgetful. Yet, Brad is so hard to pin down sometimes, it does make it difficult . . ." Her misty blue gaze settled on Samantha. "I hope all of this talk about Brad isn't boring you, dear. But, you see, when you only have one child, I'm afraid you spend too much energy worrying about him." Her eyes grew misty.

"Brad and Joel had some wonderful times together," she resumed. "Oh, there were the ordinary scrapes boys get into—but nothing serious. Brad always had lots of acquaintances, but when Joel moved to town—well, even though they were in competition often, they struck up an almost instant friendship. It was as if Brad needed somebody like Joel to give him that extra push to succeed—in grades, athletics, everything. Before he met Joel, I'm afraid Brad expected things to come too easily—and whenever they didn't, he just shrugged and said he hadn't been really interested anyway. So, you see, having Joel here to give Brad a run for his money, make him try harder, was very gratifying to me."

"I'm glad Joel was able to bring out the best in Brad," Samantha responded quietly.

"Oh, he did that all right!" Mrs. Davies said, her face brightening. "Well, that's enough reminiscing for one day. If you let me, I'll jabber on forever. But it's so nice to be able to discuss Brad with someone who knows him so well. If only he'd had time to come home before he took off for California." The older woman sighed, looking away for a moment, before her gaze returned to rest on Samantha and Joel. "Enough wishful thinking! Brad's a busy man and I shouldn't expect so much. Now, I want to hear all about you two—how you met, what kind of house you live in..."

Miss Gable proved easy to trail. Her bright red hair bounced under a fox-trimmed hat as she left the advertising agency and walked four blocks to a gleaming, modern apartment building. Samantha and Joel followed her in the car, weaving in and out of the rush-hour traffic. When the secretary disappeared into the foyer of the building, Joel pulled the car over to the curb.

"Now what, coach?" he asked.

Samantha frowned in concentration. "Well, darling, we wait for a while, I guess. Maybe we can question some of the tenants later."

"It's damned cold to be sitting out here very long, Sam," Joel retorted. "Besides, this whole thing is such a shot in the dark. There must be millions of blue-eyed women who wear a size petite. You yourself would have looked spectacular in that gown..." He looked at her speculatively, a gleam of remembrance in his eye.

"I don't think so, Joel," she offered gently. "Call it instinct or whatever, but I really think Miss Gable's our best lead. We know Brad's in California—or at least that's what he told his mother—but we need to know *exactly* where he is before we just hop on a plane and jet out to the West Coast."

Joel grimaced. "Okay," he agreed. "You're the expert."

Samantha sighed. She really wasn't sure how much more of this investigation Joel could take. He'd been silent and preoccupied after they'd left Mrs. Davies's house. She knew it must have been very painful for him to hear the woman praise his friendship with Brad. And no doubt it had been equally difficult for him to face the extent of the lies Brad had told his mother. All that business about an import-export firm offering him a job! Samantha knew she would stake every cent they owned on the proposition that Brad's "job" in California was far from legitimate.

A delivery van glided into the space in front of the car. A handsome young man in his twenties hopped out of the vehicle. He was carrying a number of large pack-ages, all bearing the name of a swank-looking department store Samantha had noticed earlier in the day. As the man went into the apartment building, the glimmer of an idea began to shine in Samantha's eyes. She tossed it around in her mind for a few minutes and then decided to follow her hunch as she saw the delivery man leave the building again.

"Be back in a minute," she said to Joel and, before he could react, she had jerked the car door quickly open, her long legs covering the distance between the street and the entrance to the apartment building in moments. As the delivery man loped down the steps, Samantha deliberately bumped into him. His shoulder grazed her full breast.

"Oh, I'm sorry!" she apologized. "Are you all right?"

The man's shameless stare of frank appreciation told her he was better than that. And he'd taken the bait. Now to make him swallow it.

"I was in such a hurry to get in out of the cold," Samantha hurried on. "Guess I should have been watch-ing what I was doing. But all I can think about is getting out of Minnesota and taking a trip to somewhere warm and sunny."

"Yeah," the delivery man agreed, pushing his billed cap back to reveal stylishly cut blond hair. "Know what you mean. I just delivered a whole load of resort wear to a good-looking redhead on the third floor. She's ob-viously getting ready to do what we're only dreaming about!"

"Miss Gable is going on a vacation?" Samantha said casually.

The man's green eyes clouded in confusion. Then they brightened. "Uh—yeah. Sally Gable, that was her name all right. Said she was going to California in the morning. Do you know her?"

"I've met her, seen her around," Samantha answered, trying to conceal her excitement.

The man nodded absently, his green gaze raking Samantha's face and figure. "Hey! I've got an idea! If you're so cold, why don't I stop by after I finish these deliveries? We can go out for a drink somewhere. That should warm you up a little." He stepped closer. "Or we could even stay at your apartment if you don't feel like getting back out in the cold..."

"Sounds like fun," Samantha answered smoothly, "but I really have a lot of work to catch up on tonight and—"

"Come on, sweetheart. All work and no play makes for a dull life." The man rested his hand on Samantha's shoulder. "Some nice music, a little wine—"

"Oh, that does sound awfully nice," Samantha answered wistfully. "But I really—"

The man slid his hand to her face, his gloved fingers caressing her cheek. "Baby, I don't like refusals and you look as if you could—"

He never finished the last sentence because a strong arm collared him from behind. "Beat it, clown!" Joel warned. "The lady's spoken for."

The delivery man wheeled around angrily. Although he was a few inches shorter than Joel, he was of heavier build. His arm shot toward Joel's face, but he hadn't counted on the taller man's agility. Joel ducked quickly, throwing the delivery man off-balance. Then, making the most of his opportunity, he brought his leg up, placing his foot squarely in the younger man's chest. It was a shove that would have put a bar-room brawler to shame.

"Get in your van and don't come back!" Joel shouted angrily as the man staggered backward onto the sidewalk. For one agonizing instant, Samantha thought the delivery man was going to continue the fight. He raised his fists menacingly, taking a few steps forward, but Joel's dark, threatening stare seemed to change his mind. The delivery man turned abruptly and got into his van, leaving a trail of burning rubber as he shot away from the curb.

"Joel!" Samantha admonished heatedly, "I was doing fine! What in the world's come over you? You could have screwed the whole thing up!"

He seized her arm and marched her back to the car. Climbing in beside her, he sat hunched over the steering wheel, breathing heavily. A small muscle in the side of his jaw twitched uncontrollably and an angry, red flush colored his face.

"We're going to sit here until both of us calm down," he spat through clenched teeth. "Then we're going to cross the street, enter that coffee shop, and you can tell me what—if anything—you found out from that delivery man."

Samantha started to inform him that he had never given her orders before, and he was not going to start doing so now—but as she twisted in her seat to focus a furious glare on Joel, he passed his hand over his face, shaking his head in disbelief. "I can't believe I lost control like that," he muttered. "The visit with Brad's mother shook me up more than I realized, I guess." He turned to face her, his eyes tinged with regret. "Enough said?"

Samantha bit her lip. Joel's self-confidence and his usually reasonable judgment had, for a few heated moments, taken a worse beating than the delivery man. "Enough said," she answered quietly, feeling a mixture of relief and sympathy. "I think having coffee sounds like a good idea."

Fortunately, the coffee shop was one that stayed open all night. Already icy temperatures plummeted to thirty degrees below zero as the day slipped into evening darkness. Samantha figured that had they sat in the car, unable to run the heater more than a few minutes every hour, they would probably have turned into ice sculptures.

She and Joel had chosen a booth near the window, from which it was easy enough to keep watch on the apartment building across the street. Despite the delivery man's report that Sally Gable wasn't leaving for California until the next morning, Samantha was afraid the secretary might change her mind and leave during the night. So, with one eye on the Highgate Apartments, and the other on Joel, Samantha told him all she'd learned from the department store delivery man.

"But I think we should still try to question a few tenants on the third floor, Joel," she said, sipping at her third cup of coffee. "And we'd better do it before it gets too late."

They paid their check and walked back across the street in a gusting, north wind. Inside the lobby, they chose the random name of a third-floor tenant from the mailbox, and picked up the lobby phone. No answer. "Mr. Paul Dawson doesn't seem to be at home," Samantha said.

"Here. Try Miss Kathryn Lansing," Joel offered. Seconds after Samantha had picked up the phone, a female voice answered. "Yes, who is it?"

"Miss Lansing, we're sorry to bother you, but we'd like to know if you've seen a man who might be my missing brother." Samantha launched into a description of Brad, elaborating her story with details that seemed to satisfy Miss Lansing, as well as to elicit the hoped-for response.

After four inquiries to third-floor residents, Samantha and Joel were able to ascertain that a man of Brad's description had been seen visiting Sally Gable. One old lady even offered the information that Brad appeared to have spent the night with the secretary recently, but that he hadn't been back over the last two days.

Samantha and Joel returned to the coffee shop, this time ordering hamburgers. As they waited for their food, Joel said, "I feel we've really made some strides, Sam.

If we can manage not to lose Sally Gable, she may lead us right to Brad."

"Yes. But, darling, when we do find him, we still have to keep a low profile. To prove beyond a shadow of a doubt that Brad stole Catwalk, we must catch him with the goods—preferably actually trading the disk in for money. That way, our case is airtight. So," she added carefully, "we can't afford to be emotional until everything is wrapped up. One slip—and Brad could be off the hook."

Joel's handsome face tensed. "I understand, Sam. You know, I've always respected your profession, your ambition to follow in your father's footsteps, but I guess I never realized how frustrating—or how personally involving detective work can be."

Samantha took his hand across the formica table. "Maybe something good will come out of this awful situation yet. Maybe we'll have gained a better understanding of each other."

Joel nodded and wearily pushed the sheen of dark hair off his forehead. "That's what it's all about, isn't it, Sam? Learning to love and live together under the best and worst of circumstances."

"Yes," she agreed softly. Encouraged by Joel's admission, she asked, "Darling, tell me, did you—perhaps subconsciously—suspect Brad, soon after Catwalk was missing?" It was a loaded question, one she might not have dared ask two days ago.

Joel's dark eyes reflected the turmoil of his inner search. "I've asked myself that a hundred times lately, Sam, and I don't have a clear answer —even for myself. But, deep down, I wonder . . . It's true that by the second day after Catwalk had disappeared, I really didn't believe it could have been just an error. But, as for suspecting Brad, or even, for that matter, Mary Beth, I couldn't seem to let myself—until the night you forced me into admitting they were the only other two people who had access to the source code." He sighed and lowered his eyes. "I kept skirting the edge of the truth, grasping at straws, telling myself the problem had to be mechanical."

Poor Joel! He depended and relied upon the essential loyalty of those to whom he was close. In fact, he'd wanted to sustain his trust badly enough that he'd done everything he could to avoid facing the truth. Samantha swallowed hard. She was afraid there was still a lot of pain ahead for Joel. In an eerie way, he would have to go through some of the same stages she'd gone through in mourning her father—disbelief, anger, grief and finally, acceptance.

Joel leaned forward, his voice an agitated whisper amid the din created by the surrounding patrons. "Brad always liked playing it close to the edge, having the thrill of seeing if he could pull certain things off. Taking chances was fun, I guess, when we were kids. In fact, I sort of admired his daring—then." He paused, seemingly lost in memory. "There was a pond—near Brad's house. The owner told us that if we wanted to skate, we had to ask permission. It was more of a safety precaution than anything else. One time, the ice was marginally thin, but Brad dared me to skate with him. I remember being tense, not only about falling through the ice, but also about the owner discovering we'd disobeyed him. Half an hour or so after we'd begun to skate, the headlights of the owner's pickup shone through the trees. We could see him winding down the drive from his house. But Brad wouldn't leave until the last minute. We came close to being caught. Brad laughed all the way back home. Coming so close to danger seemed to give him a thrill. I remember thinking how brave he was..." Joel's voice turned hard. "But it's not brave and certainly not admirable to mess with human lives, especially when you're an adult."

"I know, darling," Samantha said, realizing the words were inadequate.

"We were best buddies, almost from the time we laid eyes on one another," Joel continued softly, the bitterness in his tone gone, as he reminisced. "Here I was, a new kid in town who didn't know a single soul. On the third or fourth day after we'd arrived—I can't remember which—I was shooting baskets outside after school, and this good-looking, blond kid about my size came up and asked if he could join me. God, I was so *grateful* to have someone to play with..." Joel paused and smiled crookedly.

"I'd moved around so much I knew it was only a matter of time before I fit in, but Brad, as it turned out, was popular and his acceptance—his friendship—enabled me to become part of those tight, little junior high cliques faster than I could have on my own. We had a lot of things in common. Oh, he wasn't as interested in making good grades as I was—but that changed because of the competition between us. Most of the time, we were neck and neck. Occasionally, one or the other would come out on top, but each of us took it in stride—and just tried a little harder the next time. I've always thought of that part of my life as—challenging and special."

Samantha twirled the tips of her fingers against the smooth skin of his palm, then raised his fingers to her lips and brushed a kiss against them. "You were very lucky, darling, to have a close friend like Brad. And no matter how this investigation turns out, I hope you'll hold those memories close to your heart. People change, Joel. For whatever reasons, Brad's grown into someone very unlike the boy you knew and admired. What were attractive, boyish traits have become exaggerated into adult dishonesty. But you must not allow that to ruin your feelings about a cherished part of your past."

Joel slid his fingers down between hers and then clasped her hand tightly. "Lord, Sam, when did he turn into such a deceitful, dishonest human being?" Not waiting for an answer, he began to speak again. "You know, I saw him off and on over the years. When we got older, we'd drive all night for a special celebration or an impulsive, just-for-the-hell-of-it party. Sometimes we included other friends. Brad seemed as he always had—a little more daring than I, quicker to break the rules, faster with the lines he gave to women. But it was all part of his charm —just the way Brad happened to be. I never thought of his devil-may-care attitude as a prelude to serious deceit —or criminal behavior, for godsake!"

"No one would have, darling," Samantha assured him. "But you have to remember, Joel, you'd seen Brad infrequently over the years—until you called him about joining Hyperspace. You didn't really *know* him anymore. What you knew and felt was what you'd once shared. Those quick interludes over the years didn't really count as trust-building encounters."

"No," Joel said bitterly. "I see that now." He released her hand and picked up his coffee, taking a long sip. Placing the mug back down on the table, he mused thoughtfully, "It was all such a wonderful dream, Sam —a childhood dream come true. We'd always talked about working together one day. When Hyperspace seemed to be on solid ground at last, I couldn't wait to call Brad and invite him to join me. He was eager, too, even though he said he was very successful with the advertising agency . . ."

Samantha bent forward, her blue eyes resting lovingly on his tense face. "Joel, tell me, after Brad joined Hyperspace and you started spending entire days together, did you really feel the same way about him as you always had?"

Joel shrugged, his dark eyes roaming restlessly over the other late-night patrons of the coffee shop. "I *thought* I did. But honestly, Sam, I guess it did bother me that Brad wasn't any more settled than he'd ever been. You know we saw quite a bit of him, but there were lots of times when I made excuses for us, too. Wild parties weren't very appealing to me any longer, but they still were to Brad. A couple of times he showed up at work hung over. That angered me, but I let it go by."

"For old-times' sake?"

"Yes."

"But he was doing a good job at Hyperspace, wasn't he Joel? I never had the impression you were carrying him."

Joel shook his head adamantly. "No, Sam. As I've always told you, he's the best P.R. man I've ever had." He looked down at the table for a moment and then lifted his eyes to Samantha's. "Actually, though, I did once catch him misrepresenting something to a client."

"Was it serious?"

"Not really. Brad had juggled some figures around to make Hyperspace look a little better than it was. Later, when I asked him about it, he apologized and said he'd simply made a mistake. Then he jokingly added that I shouldn't worry about things, that I should loosen up, stop trying to be perfect all the time." Joel's mouth compressed into a thin, angry line.

Samantha sat silently watching him as he struggled with his thoughts. She hated seeing him in this kind of pain, but she also knew he would have to work through his disillusionment alone.

"I've had some real blind spots when it comes to Brad, Sam," he said suddenly. "He's a great-looking package—comes all slickly gift-wrapped with a big bow on top—and I was too interested in admiring the outside to untie the ribbon and discover that there was nothing of substance inside. God! How can I have been so blind?"

"Darling, your loyalty to old memories isn't anything to be ashamed of," Samantha said gently. "Besides, there's something to be said for having a friend close enough to cause you pain. I never put myself in that position, for a variety of reasons, but there are times when I think that kind of vulnerability makes people stronger, in the end."

Anger tinged Joel's words as he responded. "Maybe you have a point, Sam, but I'll tell you one thing—the next time I reach for my rose-colored glasses, do me a favor, will you?"

"What's that, darling?"

"Yank them off and tell me to look at things the way they really are. I've had enough of sentimentality for a while!"

— 9 —

"HOW DO YOU FEEL?" Samantha asked Joel as they swung into traffic to follow the cab Sally Gable had hailed in front of her apartment building.

"I feel," Joel said tiredly, one eye on his watch, the other on the early morning rush-hour traffic, "that Miss Gable should have booked a later flight! Sam, it's seven-thirty in the morning and we haven't had a wink of sleep!"

"What's this 'we' stuff? I distinctly saw you doze off several times in the coffee shop. I'd be saying the most scintillating things, and your head would fall back against the booth!"

Joel frowned. "Funny . . . I have no memory of that. Maybe I'm getting old. After all, I'm older than you, Sam, and that's just what we older folks do—nod off in the middle of a conversation. It doesn't matter how bewitching the speaker is."

Good. He still had his sense of humor. Samantha knew he would need it more than ever as they began what she hoped would be the last leg of their investigation. "Well, you have to admit this is sort of exciting, don't you, Joel? Just like in the movies—follow that cab!"

He turned a stubble-shaded face to her for a moment, lifted one eyebrow, and then directed his attention back to the cab a few car lengths in front of them. "Excitement and forty cents will get you a cup of coffee, Sam," he said in an amused tone.

Samantha winced. "Ugh! Don't mention coffee to a

woman who's in caffeine aftershock. Honestly, Joel, I'm never drinking coffee again after last night!"

"I'll remind you of that the next time you stagger downstairs in the morning, ready for your fix," Joel promised.

Just as they expected, the cab took the exit to the airport. While Joel returned the rental car and struggled with the luggage, Samantha discreetly followed Sally Gable. The secretary had expensive taste, Samantha noted grimly, as her quarry purchased a one-way, first-class ticket to Los Angeles. Swathed in mink from hat to coat, the woman glided toward the boarding area. Hurriedly, Samantha made arrangements for coach tickets on the same flight Sally was taking.

When Joel joined her, they hung back until the secretary was well ahead of them in line. As they entered the door of the jumbo jet, Samantha caught a glimpse of Sally turning to the left, where the first-class section was located. Quickly, Samantha and Joel headed right and collapsed into their seats in the coach area.

"I'm going to sleep all the way to California," Joel announced, yawning. "All three hours plus."

"We can afford to get some rest, darling," Samantha murmured sleepily, "because, unless Sally Gable happens to be a champion parachuter, she's stuck on this plane until it lands, the same as we are."

"Ah, you're astute, Sam," Joel answered, "very, very..." His voice drifted off and his head fell onto her shoulder.

So that she wouldn't disturb him, Samantha carefully slid a few inches down into her seat, cradling Joel's head lovingly against her breast. Within seconds, she, too, was fast asleep, her hand locked in her husband's, her blond curls mingling with Joel's dark hair.

Los Angeles International was teeming with people. Long lines wound around the area where the car-rental counters were. "This is going to take forever, Sam," Joel grumbled. "Do you still have our Miss Gable in sight?"

"Yes, darling—oh, Joel, she's headed outside! I'll bet she's taking a taxi! Come on, we're going to have to do the same."

Dragging their luggage, they pushed and shoved their way across the terminal and through revolving glass doors, where Sally Gable was getting into a taxi. Directly in front of them, another cab was just pulling in. A burly man, obviously intent on beating them to the vehicle, shot around them and jerked the door of the car open.

"Hold it!" Samantha cried. "I'm sorry, sir, but we're on official police business. We're going to have to commandeer this vehicle. Now step back, please!"

Startled, the man did as he was told without protest, blinking dazedly in the bright sunshine. Before he could change his mind, Samantha and Joel leaped into the back seat and shoved their luggage onto the floor. "You're not going to believe this," she said to the driver, "but see that cab just pulling out?"

"Yeah, I see it," the long-haired young man drawled lazily.

"Well, follow it!" Samantha ordered.

The driver turned around in his seat, taking in her flushed face. "Hey, slow down, gorgeous. You're much too tense."

"I'm going to be even more tense if you don't follow that cab—please."

As if in slow motion, the man shifted his suspiciously dilated gaze to Joel. "What's in it for me?" he asked disinterestedly.

"An extra hundred bucks," Joel stated authoritatively.

The man spun around, all signs of lethargy gone, and pulled away from the curb so fast that his passengers had to brace themselves to avoid whiplash. The cab shot into traffic, narrowly avoiding a station wagon, a small sports car, and, finally, a bus. "Whew!" Samantha gasped. "He's taking our request seriously."

Joel winked. "Money talks, Sam."

"Right," Samantha managed as the driver took a corner on two wheels. "Don't get too close—please," she cautioned.

The driver looked casually into the rearview mirror, dismissing Samantha's wide-eyed apprehension. "Cool it, okay? Just go with the flow." The cab shot up an exit ramp and weaved perilously over a bridge.

Samantha glanced helplessly at Joel. He shrugged, crinkle lines of amusement playing around his mouth. "You heard him, Sam. Now try to relax, darling—" In a stage whisper aside, he added, "Slow down, gorgeous."

Samantha rolled her eyes skyward and covered her face with her hands.

Fifty-five miles northeast of Los Angeles, the cab came to a screeching halt on a dusty road. Sally Gable's cab had taken a narrow turn-off several yards ahead, winding into a basin below. From their higher vantage point, Joel and Samantha could just make out the secretary's curvaceous figure as she undulated up the pathway to a cabin.

As Joel pressed a stack of bills into the cab driver's hand, the man tipped his cap. "Stay cool, man."

"Right," Joel nodded affably. "It was an unforgettable ride, by the way."

The slender, blond driver smiled sleepily, threw the cab in reverse to execute an about-face, and sped away in a cloud of dust.

"You know, darling," Samantha said shakily, "I was looking forward to relaxing in a nice hotel—instead, here we are in the middle of nowhere with our luggage and not a bellhop in sight!"

Joel swung the heavier pieces of luggage over his shoulder, Samantha's attempt at humor sliding right past him now that they were so near the goal of their long search. "Let's get going, Sam. Brad's got to be in that cabin." He turned and began to stalk up the road. Samantha puffed along behind him, following his dusty trail until they left the roadway to descend into a grassless stretch of rocky ground located directly above the cabin. Large manzanita shrubs and scrub mesquite provided excellent concealment.

Dropping her share of luggage on the ground, Samantha said breathlessly, "Darling, I think we're a bit overdressed for this climate!" Rivulets of perspiration streamed down her face, wispy blond curls clinging to her flushed cheeks.

Joel was already peeling off his blazer and loosening his tie. Samantha followed his example, shedding her teal jacket and unbuttoning the neck of her cream-colored silk blouse. "Isn't this country amazing?" she asked, attempting to divert Joel momentarily from their purpose. "I mean, you drive one way from Los Angeles and you're in Beverly Hills—another, and you're in Malibu—or the Pacific Ocean. But out here, you're up to your neck in rural Americana!"

Joel acknowledged her comment by shrugging casually. "Well," he said, frowning down at the scurrying movements of a salamander, "at least we won't be bogged down by too many tourists. What's our next move?"

Samantha swiped at the moisture trickling down her forehead and onto her nose. "We've got to sneak down to the cabin and listen through that open window. But that's all—no confrontations until we have Brad exactly where we want him."

"Let's do it then," Joel answered impassively.

Silently, they crept down the incline among the tangled underbrush and boulders. Overhead, nonthreatening clouds drifted in an azure sky. The little cabin had a well-tended appearance—at least on the exterior. Samantha wondered if it belonged to a city dweller who, wishing to escape the smog and hectic pace of Southern California life, saw to it that his retreat was maintained pleasantly. Wild geraniums flourished everywhere and someone had carefully planted beds of lantana, their small, aromatic clusters of flowers a colorful interruption to the drab terrain.

As Samantha and Joel hid behind a wood box a few feet from the cabin's side window, voices drifted on the sweetly scented air. "Baby, I can't believe you're finally here. It's so good to see you, touch you again—"

"It felt so good to walk out of that damned ad agency, darling. All I've been able to think about since you left Minneapolis was being with you, having that cash in our hands—free to go wherever we please, buy whatever we want..."

"We're almost there, Sally. I meet my connection tomorrow evening at Jordan Monroe's costume bash. God! I'm tired of being in this cabin, but Monroe's playing it cool. He wants to complete the deal according to his terms, in a crowded place, on his own turf...I've waited so long to pull this off. I can wait a little while longer, I guess. God! What I'd have given to see Joel's face when he realized Catwalk was gone!"

Samantha felt Joel's arm muscles tense. She shifted carefully in her crouched position and moved her hand down to where he'd rolled up his shirt sleeve, and caressed his bare flesh.

"Oh, I don't care how *he* feels about the whole thing, Brad," Sally Gable said crossly. "I just want us to be together to enjoy our good fortune. Why do you have such a thing about him anyway? As far as I'm concerned, Joel Loring was simply a means to an end. The money is the really important thing, isn't it?"

"Sure, the money's the important thing, but it also feels damned good to put one over on Joel—for a change. When we were kids, things came to him so easily. I had to work like hell to keep up—let alone beat him! But, of course, he never knew how much I resented his setting the pace. He's so sickeningly fair-minded, he actually thought our competition was healthy! Then he calls at the most opportune time—as you know, the ad agency was getting close to canning me anyway. I played on our long-time relationship, bragged a little about my abilities—and bingo! The sucker offers me a job. It was the perfect opportunity."

Samantha glanced at Joel. His mouth was grimly set, his body coiled as tightly as a spring. A muscle twitched in the side of his jaw. She stroked his arm in a silent attempt to convey her love and support. It seemed a pathetic gesture, but it was the best she could manage under the circumstances.

Just then Sally Gable's high-pitched voice assaulted their ears. "Well, darling, if you're getting some psychological kick out of this little scam, it's fine with me. But, Brad, I wonder if you know how hard it was for me to wait—all that time you were with Hyperspace—and I could only risk coming to see you that once..."

"Yeah, I felt the same way, baby. I missed you like crazy. Didn't I prove that by all the money I sent? But I couldn't afford to keep you around on a regular basis. I had to convince Joel I was the same old playboy I'd always been. Keep it mellow. Well, it worked!"

"Tell me those other women meant nothing to you, that they were just a front."

"I'll do better than that, honey. Let me convince you in the way you'll understand best..."

A few minutes passed, then Samantha silently motioned to Joel to follow her back up the hill. Once they were safely concealed behind the overgrown shrubs, she threw her arms around him. "Darling, I know how hard this must be for you, but we're so close now."

His back muscles felt rigid to her touch, his lips cool and dry beneath her own moist kiss. "Joel?"

He reached out to touch her cheek. "I'm all right, Sam. Or will be. It's just going to take some time for me to accept being used. I can't believe the resentment Brad has against me, Sam. He actually despises me because of some twisted conception... I really believed we were good for each other, that our friendship brought out the best in both of us."

He broke off and sank to the warm, hard earth. "I'm all right," he repeated.

Samantha sat down beside him, rubbing his back and tactfully remaining silent for a few minutes. Joel finally seemed to relax under the comforting kneading of her fingers. Slowly, he turned to her and smiled. "Thanks for hanging in there with me, Sam. If you weren't here, God knows I'd blow the whole case—barge in there and beat the holy hell out of Brad!"

"You'll find it much more satisfying to build an iron-clad case against him, darling—put him away for a long time." Samantha tapped her fingers along his back, thinking. "Do you know the Jordan Monroe he mentioned?"

"I don't know him personally, but I've heard of him. He's big-time, but the word is he's in trouble. The last few months he's been losing out to his major competitor."

"So he's probably desperate. Just like you suspected."

"No doubt, Sam. We're talking about a multimillion-dollar corporation that has lots of influential stockholders to answer to."

They sat together in the warm sun while Joel explained to Samantha more about the inner workings of the computer industry. She listened attentively, continuing to massage the nape of his neck and the muscles in his broad shoulders.

An hour later, Sally Gable left the cabin, walking around the back. She emerged minutes later, driving a Jeep up the narrow turn-off to the road. Samantha and Joel flattened themselves to the ground as she passed within one hundred yards of their hiding place. "We've got to find somewhere we can get cleaned up, eat, and rest for a while," Samantha said, watching the Jeep disappear over the rise. "Then we can return to keep watch on the cabin again. Brad's big deal doesn't come down until tomorrow night anyway."

"Sam, in case you've forgotten, we're not in a position to call a cab."

She stood up, dusted off her clothes, and extended a hand to Joel. "You've heard of hitchhiking, haven't you."

"Sam—" But Joel's warning went unheeded. Samantha was already heading for the road.

Half an hour later, Joel tapped his wife on the shoulder. "Honey, I don't want you to think I'm being pessimistic, but, by actual count, we've only seen five cars, none of which showed the slightest inclination to stop."

Samantha's face clouded over for a moment; then she smiled. "The next one will, darling. We've just been going about this the wrong way."

"Sam, I refuse to throw my body in front of a car."

"That won't be necessary, Joel. I've always hated clichés, but I'm about to indulge in the oldest one in the book." Samantha undid her blond topknot and let the golden curls cascade to her shoulders. Rolling the waistband of her skirt up, she effectively shortened its length by a few inches and then struck a seductive pose by the side of the road, motioning Joel to stay out of sight.

Fifteen minutes later, an old pickup came rattling along in a cloud of dust. The middle-aged driver sped past Samantha, did a double take, screeched to a stop, and ground the gears of his battered truck into reverse. Leaning out the window, he appraised Samantha sharply. Apparently more than satisfied with what he saw, he smiled. "Hi, beautiful! You in some kind of trouble?"

"I certainly am. My car's broken down back there." Samantha gestured over her shoulder, allowing the leering driver an eyeful of a well-curved breast straining against the thin material of her blouse. "I wonder if you could give me a lift to the nearest motel?"

The driver looked as if he'd just been dealt a royal flush. "Hey! No problem, honey! You just hop in here with me and—"

"I have a friend with me, too," Samantha interrupted sweetly.

The driver's grin broadened. "A friend? Where is she?"

Joel appeared from behind a large boulder. "That'd be me, pal."

The driver's expression altered visibly, but before he could change his mind, Samantha ran around the front of the pickup and jumped into the cab. To her dismay, she found herself sharing the seat with a wire cage containing a beady-eyed rooster. "Where's my friend going to sit?" she asked, shoving her suitcase between her knees.

"In back," the man stated emphatically. "You comin', mister?" he shouted out the window. "If so, hop in with them chickens!"

Joel's expression resembled a thundercloud floating on the horizon of an otherwise perfectly sunny day. "Right," he replied tersely and vaulted into the rear of the truck, where squawking chickens and an incredible aroma waited to assault his nostrils.

The farmer shifted into low gear, evidently deciding to skip second, because Joel barely had time to settle his long frame and luggage among the mesh cages before the truck began a furious clip down the road.

Twenty minutes later, the truck jerked to a stop in front of a roadside motel that looked like a leftover from the gold-rush days. Thanking the driver, who crossly ignored her sunny smile, Samantha got out of the truck and rushed around to meet Joel. Her handsome, athletic husband was in the process of limping stiffly over the tailgate. Chicken feathers were caught among the dark waves of his hair. Road grime covered his face and his clothes had a decidedly lived-in look.

Samantha's mouth quivered during her valiant attempt to keep from laughing. Joel busied himself picking chicken feathers from his hair, knocking the dust from his sports coat. Regarding her with a pointed stare, he said grimly, "Don't even think of laughing. And remind me never to suggest we move to the country, Sam. And by the way. You ought to see yourself!"

Samantha reached up to touch her wind-blown hair. Her fingers met with something soft and feathery, and she soon picked three or four chicken feathers out of the thick blond masses. Laughing, Joel helped her find several more. A quick perusal of her face in her compact mirror showed dust-streaked cheeks and forehead. "Ugh," she said. "Why'd that farmer have to drive with all the windows open?"

"Don't fret, my dear. You still got the better part of this hitchhiking experience," Joel said solemnly. "I only wish you'd had the joy of being tossed all over the back of that contraption the way I was. Ten to one, those hens all lay scrambled eggs!"

Suppressing a chuckle, Samantha meekly took his arm, and they walked slowly into the motel office. A weather-beaten, middle-aged man sat behind the desk. One look at the grimy, disheveled couple entering, and he rose to his feet, gesturing angrily. "Hey! Get outta here! I don't let rooms to hippies!"

"We are not hippies," Samantha said indignantly, fingering her tangled hair. "We're a married couple who've run into—uh—a little bad luck—and we—"

"Bull!" the proprietor roared. "If you're married to each other, I'm the Queen of Sheba! You two don't fool me none. You've been out in the wilds doing God knows what!" He sniffed the air. "I don't even want to think about what you've been doing! *You smell like chickens!*"

"Sir," Samantha began as reasonably as possible, "we want a room and—"

"Get outta here before I call the cops," the man ordered.

"Now listen," Samantha said plaintively, "we're beat. All we want is a room. If you'll just—"

"No way! I've only got one room left anyhow. The rest is filled up with rodeo riders. And I ain't gonna let you two screwballs have it!"

Joel turned to Samantha. "This is all your fault!" he shouted. "If you hadn't let the car run out of gas and forced us into a ride with that poultry farmer, none of this would be happening! I work hard all year long so we can afford a vacation to California and you ball up everything as usual!"

Samantha stared at Joel in disbelief. "Joel—"

"Don't 'Joel' me! I've had it with you! Once you got the vacation of your dreams, I thought you'd stop nagging, but no, it's just more of the same old thing!" Joel glowered at his disheveled wife, the merest twinkle offsetting his pretended anger.

By now, Samantha had received his message loud and clear. Arms on her hips, she shouted, "Mr. know-it-all! You've got eyes! Why didn't you tell me the gas tank was low? Huh? And then you used up all our fuel when you read the map wrong. It was you who got us lost out in the wilds! Now here we are—obviously in the middle of nowhere—a long way from Gucci's, buster!" She reached out and shoved Joel.

Out of the corner of her eye, Samantha saw the innkeeper's expression change. His head bobbed back and forth as he tried to keep up with the two combatants, who were getting ready for round two.

"Don't touch me! Keep your lousy hands to yourself!" Joel bellowed.

Samantha's voice grew strident. "Yeah? You and who else are going to make me?"

Joel jabbed an accusing finger in her face. "Well, I'll tell you this! If you bring that battle-axe mother of yours into this—the way you usually do—I *won't* stand a chance!"

The innkeeper rose from his chair and made his way around the counter. His once suspiciously narrow gaze was now wide with sympathy.

Samantha pretended to ignore him. Thrusting her hand at the middle of Joel's chest, she screamed belligerently, "My mother's three thousand miles away, you dolt!"

"Whoa!" the innkeeper cried. "That's enough." Turning to Joel, he said, "Mister, you've got my sympathy. If I didn't believe you two were married before, I do now. Boy! Your wife's as bad as mine! Can't do nothin' right, then blames you for her screw-ups. I'll give you a room—cash in advance, of course."

"Thanks," Joel answered, still leveling a menacing stare at Samantha, who glared back with equal fury. "It's a pleasure to do business with a man who understands the jams these damned women get us into!" He handed the red-necked innkeeper the amount specified on a hand-lettered sign hanging above the desk.

The man counted the cash carefully and then jerked his thumb to the left. "Fourth door down. Vending machine's at the end of the row. We don't have no room service here!" He laughed heartily at his own joke.

"No, I suppose not," Joel answered, managing a weak smile.

The innkeeper frowned.

Quickly, Joel added, "But we've never cared much for fancy service anyway. No, sir, give us a Coke and a candy bar and we're more than happy."

Minutes later, Samantha and Joel flopped their luggage down in a small dingy room. "Not exactly the Ritz, is it?" Joel asked, arching an eyebrow.

"No, but it's a roof over our heads and it has a shower. Oh, Joel, you were terrific!"

"You played your part pretty well, too, Sam," he conceded, drawing her into his arms. His lips moved over her dust-streaked face. "How about a shower, darling?"

"I can't think of anything I'd like better."

The water cascading over their tired bodies felt like a massage. Samantha gratefully leaned against the wall of the cramped shower stall and let the spray hit her full force. "Boy, am I glad neither of us has the jaded conception of marriage our charming innkeeper has," she said with a sigh. "What a way to go through life!"

"Some people are doomed from the start," Joel answered. He gave her a long, slow perusal, a humorous glint in his eyes. "Thank God you know your place, woman! It saves me the trouble of teaching you!"

"Oh, yeah? In that case, would you like me to do

your back, master?" Samantha asked.

Joel turned to face her, his dark eyes scanning her glistening body. "After I lather you up," he answered huskily. Taking the soap, he carefully massaged Samantha's face and neck, moving slowly down her shoulders until he reached her full breasts. Gingerly touching the soap to her velvety nipples, he covered them with opalescent bubbles, his fingers exquisitely probing the airy sparkles until each burst in succession.

"Joel," Samantha moaned. "That's so—"

"Erotic?"

"Hmmm..."

"Your turn, Sam."

She took the soap from his hands and began to work her way down his lithe body. The swirling motion of the suds against the rock-hard muscles of his chest intrigued her as her fingertips wove a tantalizing trail of bubbles around each flat, brown nipple. Harsh gasps rose in Joel's throat as Samantha gently kneaded, causing the glimmering bubbles to meld into the soapy, streaming water. "God, that *is* good," Joel said, moaning.

"A little trick I learned from my favorite tutor," Samantha murmured huskily, clasping her hands around his neck to draw his parted lips to hers. Their kiss was achingly tender at first, and then, as their need swelled, their mouths devoured each other hungrily. Joel's tongue slipped between Samantha's moist lips and drove deeply to touch the sensitive tissue on the inner reaches of her mouth. She caught her breath in short, uneven gasps.

One hand moved to Joel's dark, wet hair, threading through the heavy waves. Palming the soap in the other hand, she swirled it over his lean abdomen, a fingertip teasing his navel. Joel withdrew from the sensual exploration of her mouth and buried his lips in the sensitive hollow of her shoulder, his hands caressing her slender back, then the delicate dip between her waist and hip.

Samantha skimmed the bar of soap over the tautly stretched muscles of his upper legs, and as Joel's knee rose to taunt the throbbing pulse between her thighs, liquid fire consumed her lower belly. The soap dropped to the tiles below and her fingers moved with unerring knowledge to the swell of his masculinity. Joel lifted his head from the soft, hot hollow of her shoulder and groaned, succumbing to the aching surge of his loins.

He clasped his arms under her well-shaped buttocks. Long, slender legs entwined with his, and as he filled her with his loving desire, Samantha arched her back away from his broad chest, allowing both the jetting water and Joel's lips to linger on her breasts. It was then that the hot water ran out.

Undaunted, Joel held her to him with one arm while the other reached up to turn off the shower. Then, clasping her body tightly, he strode purposefully to the bed. Still locked in love, they fell onto the mattress, dripping wet, and consummated what they'd begun.

It wasn't as easy for Joel to convince the innkeeper to lend out his ancient car as it had been convincing him to give them the room, but when Joel slipped the cantankerous man a fifty-dollar bill, he became instantly acquiescent. "Just take good care of her. Me and Amanda's been together a long time," the proprietor warned. "And I'll need it back, the day after tomorrow. Promised the missus I'd take her into Los Angeles. You know how that goes," he added, giving Joel a conspiratorial wink.

"Certainly," Joel answered. "Never disappoint a woman who has her heart set on a night out. That's my motto."

The innkeeper grinned. "You're starting to get the hang of things, buddy. I'll bet you've even figured out that if you give in to 'em—oh, once a month or so —they won't give you as much static the next time you need a night out alone. Know what I mean?"

"Absolutely," Joel agreed, ignoring Samantha's tight-lipped smile. "Now, may I have the keys, please?"

"Sure thing. Amanda's out back—behind the office."

"Thanks," Joel said to the innkeeper, quickly steering Samantha out the door with one hand, while the other adeptly caught the keys tossed in his general direction.

Amanda turned out to be a 1955 Chevrolet that had obviously seen better days. "Think he named the car after his wife?" Samantha asked, looking at it in horror.

Joel chuckled, sliding behind the wheel of the dilapidated vehicle. "Nope. Honey, you caught a glimpse of his attitude about matrimony—my guess is he thinks too much of Amanda here to do that." He patted the steering wheel. "More likely he named this baby after a favorite pet!"

"Charming," Samantha answered, settling carefully onto the sagging seat. "Well, drive on, James. It'll be dusk soon."

Amanda backfired regularly on the way to the cabin and died twice on sharp turns. Samantha knew better than to laugh, but the sight of her husband dressed in an ecru linen sports coat, matching slacks, and an expensively tailored silk shirt, banging angrily away on the dash of the vintage vehicle, caused her to call on all her self-restraint.

Joel parked the car off the side of the road before the hill crested and they repeated the trek they'd made earlier, climbing upward until they could descend into the rocky area of shrubs to look directly down on the cabin in the basin below. The Jeep was nowhere in sight. "I wonder where our Miss Gable is," Samantha said. "I thought she might be back by now."

"I'd imagine she's ensconced in a first-rate hotel in Los Angeles, waiting for Brad to complete his deal," Joel said bitterly. "Somehow I don't see her as the rustic type."

Samantha straightened her slender shoulders. "Well, darling, let's sit down and make ourselves semi-comfortable. We should keep watch until it's late enough that we feel Brad isn't going to change his schedule. If nothing happens, we can go back to the motel and get a good night's rest."

Joel sighed and sat down beside her on the rock-strewn slope. A warm breeze stirred the air and the pale blossoms of several indigenous plants. The manzanita shrubs rustled briefly and then, as the wind died, settled back into the sentinel shape of evergreens. "It could be a long night," Joel said with yet another sigh.

Samantha leaned forward, bracing her elbows on her knees. She cupped her chin in her hands. "I'm afraid, darling, that a lot of detective work isn't very exciting. Contrary to what we see on television, there's a great deal of tedious surveillance work involved. And very few chase scenes."

"I won't argue that with you, love."

Minutes passed as they sat idly, lost in thought. "You know," Joel said, interrupting the comfortable silence between them, "I've been doing a lot of thinking about Brad. More and more pieces are starting to fall into place."

Samantha slipped her fingers inside his shirt collar, trailing them over the corded muscles of his neck. "Such as?" she asked.

"Oh, the time Brad talked me into trampling a bunch of flowers in an old lady's yard. She lived on the block behind him and had given us some static about using her lawn as a shortcut to his house. Brad decided to get even with her by ruining her petunias. I still don't know why I went along with it, except he said something about proving my loyalty to him—interesting concept, isn't it?"

"What happened?"

"The old lady didn't catch us, but I started feeling guilty. A week or so afterward, I paid her a visit, confessed, and offered to replant her flower bed. I didn't implicate Brad, of course. She was actually pretty understanding. I bought new seeds out of my allowance and took care of things. Shortly after that, Brad found out what I'd done. He got angry, accused me of being a pansy, and stalked off—but not before he got in his parting shot."

"What was that?"

Joel turned to face her, his dark eyes bright with memory. "He said, 'we got away with it. Why'd you have to go and play hero, as usual?'"

"Is that the way he thought of you? As a hero?"

Joel frowned down at the soil. "I don't really know. Maybe. He used to tease me a lot about always wanting to be 'the guy in the white hat.' But I never paid much attention to his comments. You know how kids are— always razzing each other. And I wasn't a goody two shoes, by any means. But looking back, I'd have to say I was essentially more up-front than Brad. He had a way of getting around things without being totally dishonest or telling a blatant lie."

"He dissembled—sort of changed the facts so they were in his favor?"

"Exactly." Joel's brow furrowed in thought. "Like the time we were in college. I skipped classes one Friday— drove all day so I could attend a big party Brad's fraternity was having that night—even took a carload of friends along. We had the usual, wild time—too much drinking, a lot of carrying on. Anyway, after the party, we ended up at a local guy's house. His parents were out of town. There were girls present, naturally. I sort of came on to one girl, who seemed to reciprocate my interest. When Brad noticed our friendliness, he pulled me over to one side and informed me the girl and he had just broken up and he didn't want to see me get caught up in her rebound reaction."

"So what happened?"

"I left her alone the rest of the evening. But the next day I learned inadvertently from one of Brad's fraternity brothers that she and Brad had split up several weeks before—*her* idea."

Samantha lifted her hand from Joel's neck and slid her arm around his shoulders. "Did you ever confront Brad with the information?"

"No. There didn't seem to be any point and I didn't really give it serious thought—until now." Joel reached over to straighten a tortoise-shell comb in her hair. "Maybe none of these old memories is very important, but they sure keep popping to the surface a lot lately."

"I think they are important, Joel. The isolated incidents don't mean much by themselves, but knowing what we do now, they help round out the picture. I think our friend Brad has a long history of devious, jealous behavior—especially where you're concerned."

Joel started to respond when they heard the sound of a car below, moving along a back road that wound through the foothills. It circled the rear of the cabin and stopped in front of the structure. A middle-aged, well-dressed man got out and entered the door without knocking. "Oh, boy!" Samantha exclaimed. "Time to get to work."

"What do we need to do, Sam?" Joel asked. "Sneak down there to listen?"

She rose gracefully, pulling Joel up with her. "Darling," she said carefully, "I'm going to have to sneak down there by myself to see if anything important is going on. If necessary, I may tape the conversation between Brad and that man. I'm going to have to ask you to stay here and keep watch, in case someone else shows up. You've got to be in a position to warn me if that happens."

"Sam, I don't like the idea of your being down there alone. It'll be dark soon, and I'm sure Brad's capable of anything—"

She placed a fingertip to his lips. "I'm the detective. Remember? I can handle myself. You really will do me more good by standing guard. Now, listen, we've got flashlights in the backpack and if I should get into any real difficulty, I'll switch mine on and off three times. Okay? And if you see anyone coming, do the same for me."

Samantha's blue eyes traveled over Joel's face. In the sunset, they looked almost amethyst. "Darling, another thing. If we should—" She paused. "If we should be separated somehow, I'll meet you at the Monroe mansion tomorrow evening. That's where this whole thing is going to culminate."

He seized her shoulders. "Sam, I have no intention of being separated from you. That's crazy, not to mention dangerous! Why are we discussing this?"

"Joel," she answered patiently, "we can't control all of the odds and it's far better to have a plan than not. Okay? I just want to make sure all of our bases are covered. Chances are this conversation is superfluous, but my father taught me always to be prepared for the unexpected."

Joel cupped his palms on either side of her face. "Don't take any unnecessary chances, Sam. Promise?"

"I'll do my best," she breathed, her voice a whisper in the twilight. "But, Joel, let's not allow our emotions to foul up this case. We've got to be patient—no matter what. Concrete evidence is what we're after. It's the only way we can be assured of nailing Brad." She retrieved the flashlight and a few other items from the backpack.

After kissing Joel quickly, she crept down the hill. When she reached the bottom of the incline, she moved stealthily behind the wood box. After a few minutes, and no sound from inside, she crawled nearer to the window.

Raising herself carefully on her knees, she peered inside. The man who had just arrived was sitting on the sofa. A portfolio rested on his knees. Brad came into the room carrying two glasses of amber-colored liquid. The stranger refused his.

"I won't be staying long, Mr. Davies. As I told you before, I'm merely an emissary for Mr. Monroe. He simply wants to confirm our arrangements."

Brad lifted the glass to his lips, took a long sip, and set the drink down on the coffee table. "No problem. I'll be there with the merchandise."

"You do have it with you?"

Brad fixed his cool, blue-eyed gaze on the stranger. "I'll have it with me tomorrow evening."

"I see. Very well. Then there would be no chance of Mr. Monroe checking out the merchandise before your appointment with him?"

"Absolutely not."

The stranger rose, clutching his portfolio. "I'll relay your message to Mr. Monroe. Thank you for your time."

Samantha heard the front door close and the sound of the car turning around. She flattened herself against the ground as the vehicle came around the far side of the cabin and sped up the back road several yards from the rear of the structure. She lay there a few seconds longer until she was certain the stranger was gone for good. Swell! She hadn't even needed her tape recorder. None of the conversation would be admissible in court.

Sticking the tape recorder in her shoulder bag, she balanced the flashlight carefully in her hand. The light was starting to fade as she gingerly rose from her prone position to a half-crouch. She'd taken only a few small strides when suddenly, she stopped. Loping toward her was a huge German shepherd. It had apparently wandered around from the rear of the cabin.

Terrific! Samantha thought. I hope you're friendly, boy. Tentatively, she stretched out her hand to pet the animal, hoping frantically he would accept the gesture and then lope off in another direction. But the moment her fingertips stroked his muzzle, a low growl escaped from the canine.

Samantha froze. The dog and she were only a few feet away from the open window of the cabin. Had Brad heard? Her question was answered in a split second. A familiar voice came from the window. "Well, well, what have you caught for me, Conrad? A private eye?"

Samantha made up her mind quickly. The flashlight rested in her hand, but she did not switch it on. This was no time to call in Joel. She straightened and took a step toward the window. The dog moved with her.

"If you'll call off this hound, I'll come inside, Brad," she said quietly.

His icy blue stare met Samantha's wide-eyed gaze. "You're coming inside one way or another. But if you prefer to do it under your own steam, come around back —slowly. The dog will follow you. He won't attack if you don't make any sudden moves."

She walked carefully toward the back of the cabin with the dog on her heels. The last rose-gold reflections of the setting sun fanned like fingertips against the sky as she approached the rear of the cabin. The door swung open, and without hesitation, Samantha stepped into Brad Davies's arms. The dog followed her in and watched the couple, menacingly.

10

THE PRESSURE OF Brad's lips against her own felt foreign, unwanted. But Samantha kissed him back with fervor. Then, as he stepped away from her, a low, grating laugh burst from his throat. "Pretty damned convincing, Samantha! You're a clever woman. But, of course, I always knew that. Tell me, off the record, how you figured out what I was up to."

"I've watched you, Brad," Samantha returned huskily. "Maybe Joel wasn't perceptive enough to catch a glimpse of the real you, but I was. I know ambition when I see it."

"Do you now? And what did I do that gave me away?" Brad moved toward her, his pale blue eyes taking on a menacing quality in the dim light.

Samantha leaned casually against the wood-trimmed sofa. "Oh, you didn't slip up, if that's what you mean. Your plan was pretty foolproof, actually. But when Joel discovered Catwalk's loss wasn't the result of a mechanical error, I knew immediately who had stolen the game. You're the only one in Hyperspace with enough ambition and know-how to pull off something like this."

She laughed throatily. "God, Brad! You've got nerve, I'll say that for you. Coming to our party right *after* you'd stolen Catwalk. You do like playing it close to the edge, don't you? But, at the same time, you walk a careful tightrope. If you hadn't come to the party, it would have aroused undue suspicion. And you read Joel like a book. You knew you could bank on his deep-seated trust of you, your long friendship. No doubt, you figured you had at least a couple of days before he suspected you—maybe longer—if Mary Beth hadn't had such a good alibi..."

"So you admire my cleverness, Samantha?" Brad asked casually, but there was an underlying tone of bitterness in his question. "You approve of the fact that I finally took something away from Joel with very little effort?"

He crossed the room quickly, forcing her chin up so that her blue gaze met his unblinkingly. "Do you?" he asked roughly.

Samantha shrugged. "Is that the important part, Brad? I would have thought the money was your motivation. After all, we're talking about a large sum, I suspect."

His hand left her chin and he began to pace about the small room. "The money is very important, Samantha. And I'll make enough that I'll never have to work again if I invest it properly. But I also get a real pleasure out of putting one over on Joel. I'd be dishonest if I didn't admit it."

He stopped walking and whirled about to face her again. "You see, Joel and I have what you might call a love/hate relationship—although the love's all on his side and the hate's on mine. Oh, I didn't always dislike him. In fact, we were pretty good friends back when we were kids. Even though I got tired of my mother throwing him up to me all the time. But as we grew older and visited or phoned each other, I got pretty sick of hearing about his accomplishments. He became like a shadow I couldn't shake—even though I didn't see him much."

Brad paused to light a cigarette. "My own life hasn't gone nearly so smoothly as Joel's. I was kicked out of college a couple of times and I lost my spot on the basketball team because of not being what the coach called a 'team player.' That's when my grades really went downhill. Joel doesn't know any of this."

"So when he called to ask you to join Hyperspace, it

seemed like the perfect opportunity to get even with him?" Samantha asked.

"Sure. Not only that, but I was on the verge of being fired from the agency. Hell! I was the best man they had. However, they suspected I'd indulged in a little 'profit sharing' off and on. Nobody had proved I'd skimmed any off the top, but they were getting close. Joel appeared with his suggestion that we realize our childhood dream of working together, at just the right time." Brad sneered. "The only trouble with his plan was that he was still on top—in charge—head Fred. So once again I got to play second best."

Samantha moved toward Brad. "I see. You *are* ambitious. You're so unlike Joel. He gets places, but it takes him so damned long. Everything has to be done honestly, fairly . . ." She touched Brad's face, tracing a line along his cheekbone. "You've only seen me with Joel. So perhaps you don't realize how impatient *I* am, how ambitious."

Brad jerked his face away from her, every muscle in his body tensing. When he spoke, his voice was low, threatening. "Speaking of Joel, Samantha—where is our Boy Scout friend? Waiting outside the cabin with the cavalry?"

She shook her head adamantly. Blond tendrils escaped around her face. "Not a chance. He doesn't know where I am."

"You expect me to believe that?"

"That's up to you. But think about it. Do you really think I'd be speaking the way I have if Joel were nearby? My God, Brad, you're smarter than that."

She waited as Brad fixed her with his piercing stare. "Does he know I'm the one who stole Catwalk?"

Samantha nodded. "Yes. That's why we came to California. But I ditched him a few hours ago. I left our hotel in Los Angeles to go on an 'errand' and simply didn't return."

Brad's hand shot out and seized a fistful of her blond hair. "I wonder how Joel would react if he knew I was about to make love to his precious wife."

Samantha covered his hand with her own, tilting her head even farther back, exposing the regal lines of her neck, a hint of cleavage peeking above the open collar of her blouse. "Just the way you'd want him to, no doubt. But before we make a move toward the bedroom, Brad, there's something we have to get straight first."

He tightened his grip on her blond curls, jerking her face savagely closer to his. "Oh, yeah? What's that?"

Samantha's lips parted. They were almost touching Brad's. "I want in on the deal. Fifty-fifty."

Joel peered anxiously into the darkness. Where in the hell was Samantha? The California sunset had faded into darkness so quickly, he'd lost sight of her slender form minutes after she'd crouched behind the wood box. The visitor to the cabin had long since left. Raising his wrist, Joel checked the illuminated dial of his watch. She'd been gone over half an hour!

Well, he wasn't waiting any longer. Miss Gable could return and surprise them if she wanted. So could any other conspirators! They would be no match for him, not in his present mood. He was concerned for Samantha's safety, and tired of playing cat-and-mouse games with Brad. If he had to, he'd physically force a confession from that crook!

Feeling his way in the darkness down the hill, Joel threaded his way among the boulders and large shrubs, moving toward the lighted patch of window. Inching along, he found the base of the hill and realized he could see more clearly in the reflected glow of the cabin. He crept to the wood box. No Samantha!

And then the sound of her voice, floating out the open window, came to him in the night air. "I've thought about this for a long time, Brad. And I simply can't fight it any longer. You're the one I want, not Joel. He lacks your ambition. When I figured out what was going on, I trailed you here..."

Joel gripped the edge of the wood box. The words gave him pause, even though he knew Samantha was putting on an act. She must be in danger, was his next thought. He'd known it might come to this, of course, but it was still a shock to realize his wife was inside the cabin with a man he considered very threatening. Had she been caught or had she chosen to meet Brad face to face?

"Samantha," Brad said icily, "I may be a lot of things, but I'm no fool. If you're on the up and up, you're going to have to prove it to me."

"I'll be happy to. But don't underestimate me, Brad. I'm not a fool either. If we're going to be a team, I want to know exactly how this deal is going to benefit *both* of us."

Smart, Joel thought. She's talking the kind of arrangement that'll be most convincing to Brad. He'd never buy her undying love for him as her principal motivation in following him.

Brad's derisive laugh echoed through the air. "You seem to forget, sweetheart, that I've got all the marbles in this little game. You're in no position to demand anything."

Joel stiffened. *Dangerous.* Sam, be careful. He bent forward, resting his weight on one heel, ready to spring into action if necessary.

His wife's lilting laugh caught his attention. "Brad, do you honestly think I'd take a chance that wasn't calculated? I'm more like you than you know. I've made certain arrangements to guarantee my safety."

"You really expect me to fall for that?" Brad asked, his voice rising dangerously.

"It doesn't matter if you believe me or not, Brad. But I think you must know I'm not stupid. And I'm used to dealing with criminals, so I'm accustomed to protecting myself. Look, why don't you just tell me what I can expect to get out of this? I'm willing to negotiate, and we both know we're attracted to one another. If we can strike up a financial bargain, we've got a hell of a future together."

"You talk a good game, lady. But if you're so smart, you must also know I'm sort of committed to a certain redhead who's supposed to meet me tomorrow night— after the deal goes down. I've already invested a lot of money in her. And I don't think you're the kind of woman who's interested in being part of a threesome, are you?"

"Definitely not. But I'll tell you what. Let's get out of this cabin, go someplace where your redheaded friend isn't liable to barge in on us. And then maybe I can convince you to change your mind about including her in this little scheme. If not, so be it. I'll drop my financial demands and be on my way. Neither of us will really have lost anything."

Joel shifted his weight, moving stealthily toward the window. What in the hell was Samantha trying to do? And then, as if in answer to his unspoken query, she spoke again in husky, seductive tones.

"Come on, Brad. Let's have a drink to new beginnings and then go to a nice hotel in Los Angeles or Beverly Hills—wherever. We've got all night and most of tomorrow to get to really know each other. What do you have to lose?"

Joel raised himself carefully from his crouched position under the window, angling his head so he could see into the cabin's living room. And then he froze.

Samantha, her lovely face tipped away from him, stood in the protection of his former friend's embrace. As Joel watched, Brad's lips claimed hers in a hungry, demanding kiss. The two clung tightly together, their blond heads shining in the lamplight. A hot bubble of rage burst in Joel's throat. He looked away for a moment and then forced his gaze back to the scene inside.

Samantha stepped out of Brad's arms. "How about that drink? I'm anxious to get on the road, find a luxurious room where"—her voice rose slightly—"*nobody* will interfere with us."

Joel got her message—loud and clear. Samantha had something up her sleeve. It was something for which she wanted no help—at least not now.

Twenty minutes later, Brad, Samantha, and a large, mean-looking German shepherd that Joel had noticed lurking around the bungalow before, got into a late-model car parked several yards behind the cabin. Joel watched as they headed up the back road that wound into the foothills. He figured the route must be a shortcut to a major freeway. Slowly, he crawled free of the tangled underbrush where he'd hidden as soon as Brad and Samantha had finished their drinks. There was no use in dashing up the hill, leaping into Amanda, and trying to pick up their trail. They'd be long gone.

All he could follow now was his part of the plan, hang loose, and meet up with Samantha at the costume party tomorrow evening. That is, if nothing went wrong. But until then . . . A dozen thoughts flickered through his head, most of them painting an unbearable picture of his wife and Brad together in some damned hotel room!

How in the hell was she going to keep Brad from taking her to bed? If she refused his attentions, Brad would certainly be suspicious. From what Joel had heard and seen in the cabin, he knew Brad would not be easily stalled or deterred from getting everything he wanted. Only Samantha could control what might take place between herself and Brad.

There was nothing he could do but trust that her professional expertise and quick thinking would keep her safe. God, this was torture! He'd never felt so helpless in his life. Only his belief in Samantha's judgment, and her repeated warnings about not allowing his emotional reactions to blow the case, had kept him from charging into the cabin to rescue his wife.

He passed a hand over his forehead, telling himself to get on with searching the cabin. Samantha couldn't have had the opportunity. Digging into the backpack, he retrieved a flashlight, shining it boldly on the deserted cabin. As he approached the front door, he gave it a nasty shove to help vent his turbulent emotions. Swinging the flashlight about, he located a switchplate. With a deft motion of his free hand, he clicked the light on and the room was instantly bathed in a yellow warmth.

He stalked across the bare floor to a closed door off the main room of the cabin. Ripping it open, he hit the light switch. Aside from a rumpled bed and an empty chest of drawers, there was very little else in the room. Disgusted, he gave the tiny, adjoining bathroom a cursory check. The only things Brad had left behind were wet towels.

There was one room left to search—the kitchen. Joel found the remnants of a half-eaten dinner and an empty fifth of Scotch. Two glasses, their contents drained, rested on the small table. Joel sank into a cane-back chair and drummed his fingers on the wood surface in front of him, staring at the glass that bore a slight smudge of lipstick on its rim. This had sure turned out to be one hell of a mess! Here he was in some godforsaken cabin in rural California, worried sick about his wife...

Brad was a clever, attractive man. He'd already proved himself an extraordinary manipulator as well as a devious criminal. Was Samantha really capable of handling him? How far would she have to go to gain his trust? Exactly what plan did she have in that beautiful head of hers anyway? She was too smart to have gotten herself into a non-negotiable position—wasn't she?

But her profession was an essential part of her life. At what point would she draw the line before she gave up on a case? What price might she be willing to pay to insure a successful resolution? Private investigation was an unorthodox profession. Perhaps it demanded unusual sacrifices or decisions in some cases. Ones she'd never cared to discuss with him.

He stood up, pacing around the kitchen like a caged animal. His thoughts seemed to be swimming in whirlpools of confusion. There was no doubt that Brad's defection had disillusioned him to the point of questioning his own perception of trust. From time to time during the investigation, he'd even allowed some of that disillusionment to spill over into his relationship with Samantha. Was that happening now? Were his mental processes so jumbled that his fear for his wife's safety might be more accurately translated into distrust of her motives?

With a sudden urge to inflict pain, Joel slammed his fist down on the countertop. Something rolled off the soap dish next to the faucet, with a metallic clink as it struck the porcelain sink below. Slowly, Joel retrieved the object. Samantha's wedding band! He walked back over to the table and placed the ring on the wooden surface. The gold shone dully in the harsh light of the exposed bulb overhead. The band conjured up memories so deeply entrenched in his heart, he couldn't will them away.

He saw Samantha as vividly as if she stood before him, the wind in her streaming, golden hair, her enormous blue eyes reflecting the light of her love for him as they jogged along a path in the park. That vision faded slowly, replaced by a memory so keen he could taste and smell the honey scent of her skin, feel the generous curve of her mouth, experience the sensation of her slender fingers caressing him in the rose-shaded bedroom in their home. And then the ecstasy of their mutual surrender coursed through him in waves of agonizing reminiscence. Doubled over as if in physical pain, Joel clutched his stomach. As if to taunt him further, his brain registered the sweet bubble of Samantha's laughter, the comic tone of her voice as she teased him, the crisp inflection in her words as she made an intelligent observation...

He picked the ring up carefully, placing it in the breast pocket of his sports coat. The gold band was a talisman! It had to be. Samantha had left it in the kitchen soap dish, a place where she must have relied upon his looking. She was always joking that he never passed a soap dish he didn't try. His father's military obsession with orderliness and cleanliness was responsible for his own addiction to soap and water. It was the most logical place for Samantha to leave the ring. She'd probably picked the kitchen because he might have overlooked the dingy little bathroom.

Thank God he'd found the ring! It had been exactly the symbolic reassurance his battered senses needed. He placed his hand on the outside of his coat pocket, comforted by the hard, unyielding circlet that pressed against the material. Somehow the ring's presence was helping him break through the haze of his pain and distrust. Whatever Samantha was doing, she was doing for him— for them. She must be. Consummate actress, mistress of illusion in her profession, she was still the woman he knew best in the world and that knowledge rested in his heart, next to where the band lay that bound their lives together.

—11—

JOEL EASED THE sputtering Amanda up the winding drive of Jordan Monroe's Spanish-style mansion. Palm trees fluttered in the early evening breeze and the tangy scents of the nearby Pacific floated through the open car window. Bordering the spacious lawn were several varieties of tropical plants, a few of which were still in colorful bloom.

At the top of the drive, parking valets in stiffly pressed uniforms were assisting the lavishly costumed guests with their cars. Mary Queen of Scots swept up the red-tiled steps, her full skirts dragging behind her. Ben Franklin, complete with gold-rimmed spectacles perched on his nose, appeared to be her escort, although he was keeping a deferential distance from her majesty.

Waving aside an eager parking valet, Joel called out, "I'll handle this old beauty myself, son. She's an authentic classic, as you can see." The gangly youth gaped as Joel masterfully swung a reluctant Amanda into a narrow spot beside a sleek new Jaguar.

After several dying gasps, the aged Chevy lurched to a complete stop. Joel got out, adjusted the black mask he'd bought in a Los Angeles Woolworths, and strode purposefully toward the glittering lights of the mansion. Inside, the party appeared to have gotten off to an early start. People mingled in the hall, already tipsy from champagne. A stiff-lipped butler, dressed as a footman, bowed ceremoniously as Joel passed. "Good evening, sir. Will Tonto be joining you shortly?"

Joel hooked his thumbs in the belt of the dime-store holster and tugged indiscreetly at the tight, all-white Western pants he'd borrowed from a rodeo rider at the motel. He shook his head. "Nope, pardner, I'm afraid he'll be staying outside. He's keeping an eye on Silver."

"Very good, sir," the butler replied formally, his face still set in pompous composure. Gesturing pretentiously down the long hall, he indicated with a flick of his finger a room on the left. "The party's supposed to be confined to the main ballroom," he said emphatically, glancing with obvious disdain at the spillover of guests surrounding them.

"Thanks, pardner. Tell you what—I'll try to sneak you a silver bullet on my way out," Joel promised as he swaggered past.

An orchestra occupied the far corner of the elegant ballroom and a food-laden buffet table ran the entire length of the opposite wall. A maid in a mermaid's costume, the finned bottom slit into a flounce so she could just barely slink along, offered Joel a glass of champagne from a sterling tray. "Let me guess," she said coyly. "You're—I've got it—the Lone Ranger!"

Joel swept his hat from his head in one smooth motion and then, arm and Stetson at his waist, he bowed. "At your service, ma'am."

"Oh, I hope so." The flirtatious maid giggled. " I have a break in an hour. Look me up and we'll go outside. You can give me a riding lesson—or something."

"Or something," Joel assured her, watching her wiggle off toward an overly fat Peter Pan.

He scanned the crowd, figuring there must be at least three hundred guests jammed into the room. How in the hell was he going to find Samantha in this crush?

His eyes settled on a tall woman, waltzing about the floor in a medieval costume, the peaked hat and veil obscuring her face and hair. Her partner was dressed in a flowing black cape and a vampire's mask, but the light gleam of his hair was still visible. Joel began to inch his way through the swirling couples, his attention fixed on the graceful duo several feet away. Just as he came within earshot of them, the woman spoke loudly above the strains of the music. "Nice bash, isn't it?"

The vampire bent his head to answer. "Yeah. Jordan always throws a mean party."

Neither voice belonged to Samantha nor Brad. Joel turned away. This was going to be even harder than he'd imagined. Jordan Monroe's mansion was a madhouse of activity. Nobody was who he or she appeared. Sights and sounds seemed confused, mingled among the strident, Mardi Gras atmosphere. I've got to find her, Joel thought, or at least catch sight of her. His concern for his wife's safety had grown steadily throughout the day.

That afternoon, he'd actually felt an upswing of confidence as he'd borrowed clothes from the rodeo rider at the motel. His optimistic belief in Samantha's professional capabilities buoyed him through the trip back to Los Angeles, the stop at a service station to look up Jordan Monroe's exclusive address in a telephone directory, the winding, unfamiliar drive through expensive neighborhoods that bordered one another in a twisting maze.

Joel decided to walk through the ballroom, covering every square inch of it if necessary. With renewed determination, he made his way slowly through the swaying dancers and clusters of animated conversationalists.

There were lots of tall, slender, blond women among the masqueraders—and that didn't begin to take into account those whose hair was hidden by elaborate headpieces.

He'd walked back and forth over one-half of the ballroom when a bosomy Pink Panther approached him. "Hi, ho, Silver! You unattached?"

"For the time being."

"Then how about a dance?" Two brown eyes, behind the slits in the mask, appraised Joel's muscular thighs, tightly sheathed in the white Western pants.

"I'll sure keep that in mind for later, brown eyes," Joel answered. "Right now, I'm afraid I'm looking for my date—lost her in the crowd. She's an old family friend and if I don't pay some attention to her, I'm going to be in trouble."

"Such a pity," the Pink Panther replied wistfully, stroking a nylon whisker. "What'd she come as?"

"Well, that's sort of hard to answer," Joel hedged. He tried to think. What would Samantha be wearing? "She likes cats," he said absently.

"Oh! She must be Garfield! I saw her earlier. She's too tall for her costume. The legs are too short and—"

"It's a ridiculous costume," Joel agreed, concealing his excitement. He bent closer to the Pink Panther, resting his hand on her shoulder. "Where'd you see her last?" he asked casually.

"Hmmm . . . about fifteen or twenty minutes ago I saw her sneaking upstairs." Her whiskers twitched as she chuckled. "Probably got an offer she couldn't refuse."

"No doubt. But I probably ought to check on her—and then if she's happily occupied, I'll rush on back to you."

The Pink Panther swatted him playfully with her paw. "Aw, don't bother with Garfield. She's a big girl. Anyway, if you get caught upstairs, there'll be a lot of trouble. Mr. Monroe always insists that his guests stay on the main floor."

Joel pretended to look shocked. "Well, in that case, I'd really better get a move on. If she gets in trouble, I'll be blamed."

The Pink Panther gave his cheek a kitten's caress. "All right, sugar, but hurry back, you hear?"

"Right," Joel said. "Shouldn't take long." He turned abruptly and strode out of the ballroom, jostling startled guests as he elbowed his way into the marble hall. The butler had his back to him as he welcomed latecomers, and Joel seized the opportunity to dash up the spiral staircase at the far end of the corridor.

This part of the house was obviously intended to be off limits to guests. The doors to all the rooms were closed and only a few lights burned in the winding passages. Joel ripped his mask off and stuffed it in his pocket. He stood motionless for several moments, but the only sounds he could hear were those of the revelry downstairs. If he had to, he'd open every door on the damned second floor until he found his wife!

Samantha adjusted the recording device and tried unsuccessfully to shift to a more comfortable position. Her knees were beginning to ache from crouching behind the door of the bathroom, which was slightly ajar. If she could hold out for just a few more minutes, she'd not only have the proof of Brad's defection on tape, she'd also be witness to the actual exchange of Catwalk for money.

She peered cautiously through the door into the adjoining bedroom. This whole thing was taking too long! Jordan Monroe had now insisted on running the Catwalk disk on the computer. Brad, appropriately attired in a devil's costume, was his usual glib, persuasive self, but Monroe was holding out until he'd satisfied himself of Catwalk's worth. Finally, the two men decided each really had something the other wanted. Catwalk was put into the computer on the desk, run through its paces, and then the conspirators got down to the business of haggling. Samantha steadied her camera, waiting...

Jordan Monroe, a heavyset, middle-aged man, leaned heavily against the desk. "Looks as if your little game is damned near everything you claimed it to be, Davies. Of course, it still has a few bugs that need ironing out."

Brad snorted. "You knew that from the beginning, Monroe. I've been straight with you about Catwalk. Sure, it's in need of a little polishing, but you've got a hundred programmers who could pull that off and have it ready to market in no time."

"True," Monroe agreed, raising two fingertips to his chin. He stood thinking for a minute, then clapped his hands together. "All right! I'll meet your price."

"Good. I thought you would," Brad answered smugly. "This is going to make us both rich men, Monroe."

Samantha watched as Monroe handed Brad a portfolio, which he opened, carefully examining the contents. A satisfied grin spread over his face, and he obligingly placed the disk in the older man's hands. Samantha silently clicked her camera.

And then the door opened quietly. Samantha tensed. She opened her mouth with a gasp of surprise as Joel strode into the room. "Good evening, gentlemen. What do we have going on here? A sales meeting?"

"I thought you said you were in this alone, Davies!" Monroe shouted.

An angry red flush stained Brad's face. He opened his mouth to speak, but Joel held up a warning hand. "Mr. Monroe, I think what you and Brad have experienced is popularly known as a failure to communicate. If you're interested in buying Catwalk, you'll have to negotiate with me. You see, I'm the inventor."

"Damn you, Joel! I should have known—" Brad cried furiously. "I can't believe it. I underestimated you. Again."

"It's always been a problem of yours, Brad—not being able to read the competition," Joel said casually.

Jordan Monroe's head pivoted back and forth between the men. "What in the hell is this?" he demanded, obviously shaken.

Joel moved toward the two men. "Brad's dealing in stolen property, Monroe. Or didn't you know that?"

"Of course he knew that!" Brad sputtered.

"Taking one hell of a risk, aren't you, Monroe?" Joel asked. "There's a heavy rap for industrial sabotage. Now, on the other hand, if we want to keep things perfectly legal, the two of us could negotiate. I'm interested in selling Catwalk to you—probably more cheaply than Brad. After all, you've got a much bigger company than Hyperspace, more facilities for marketing the game. I think we could strike a bargain that would be satisfactory to both of us."

Samantha's pulse raced with excitement. Joel was taking a terrible risk, but his ploy was brilliant! Oh, what a resourceful man she had married!

And then she saw Brad reach inside his devil's cape. She gasped as his hand whipped out in one fluid motion. In it was a gun. "Freeze! Both of you! Now get over there—into the closet."

Samantha watched with agonized dismay as Joel and a florid-faced Monroe started to back slowly toward the door in the far corner of the room. Brad had his back to her, the gun pointed at the two other men. Seizing her chance, she moved swiftly through the bathroom door, the Garfield mask shoved on top of her head, her own gun—the one she never worked dangerous assignments without—aimed squarely at the trio. Joel and Monroe saw her over Brad's shoulder.

"What?" Monroe uttered.

Brad whirled around. "Not another move!" she ordered. "Drop your gun, Brad! Now!"

His face paled. "Samantha! How in the hell did you get loose?"

"Never mind that. Put your gun down!"

Brad slowly laid the gun on the bed. Samantha kept her own weapon trained on all three men. "Stay where you are," she commanded.

Joel raised a heavy, dark brow. "Does that include the Lone Ranger, too?"

The intensity of the moment hung in the air between them. Brad and Monroe eyed her questioningly. And then like sunshine breaking through storm clouds, Samantha smiled. "Oh, no, darling. The Lone Ranger stands for truth and justice. You're the only good guy in the bunch."

Joel's relieved grin made her knees turn to jelly. He had just started toward her when the door to the room was abruptly thrown open and the Pink Panther wandered in. "There you are!" she exclaimed. "Where've you been? I got tired of—"

Brad lunged for the gun on the bed. The Pink Panther screamed. Samantha pivoted on one foot, trying to get a clear bead on Brad, but the hysterical Pink Panther stood between them. Monroe made a dash for the door, clutching the Catwalk disk to his burly body.

Joel raced after him, Samantha on his heels. They flew through the semi-darkened corridor, the sound of Brad's reverberating footsteps behind them. Monroe and his two uninvited guests hit the landing at full speed, taking the stairs to the main hall in giant leaps. Brad's gun exploded against a stucco wall. Screams of terror reverberated through the cavernous room as revelers stared in horror, at first paralyzed by the scene unfolding before them. Then, as if in waves, Mr. T.'s, Yodas, Hans Solos, Princess Leias, and a host of others dived for cover, flattening their bodies along the marbled hall.

Joel dodged and darted adeptly among the prone forms, throwing a tackle on Monroe as he tried to reach the front door of the mansion. Samantha whirled around and leveled her gun on Brad. He had just reached the bottom of the stairs. "It's over!" she cried. "Throw down your gun!"

"Like hell I will!" he answered. "Do you want to see a lot of innocent people hurt? If not, I suggest *you* drop your gun—or do you want a shootout?" His handsome face sneered down at her.

Suddenly, the door to the mansion burst open and six policemen charged into the hall, guns drawn.

Joel and Samantha stood apart on the lawn outside the Monroe mansion, the revolving lights of the police cars patterning their faces in mottled red. Overhead, a saffron-yellow moon moved slowly across the sky. Palm trees swayed in the mild night breeze, their dark whispering lost amid the cacophony of police radios and the agitated conversations of the gathered crowd.

Joel massaged an aching rib he'd bruised when he'd tackled Monroe. His eyes were on Samantha, who was being interrogated by a police officer. Brad and Monroe were already in the back seat of the squad car. Funny . . . Joel had been anticipating the triumph of this moment for days, but now that it was here, there seemed little to savor—except for the fact that Samantha was safe, and still his wife.

Several party-goers clustered around him. They were in a state of subdued excitement. Once the police had everything under control, and Brad and Monroe had been taken into custody, the guests had flocked to Joel, besieging him with questions, which he'd answered as patiently as he could.

"So Garfield's really your *wife?*" the Pink Panther asked in disappointment.

Joel smiled. "Yes—*and* a private investigator," he added proudly.

One of the five Mr. T.'s stepped forward. "I've never seen so much excitement at one of Jordan's parties before. My golf buddies aren't going to believe this!"

Darth Vader laughed, his long, black cloak rippling in the late-night air. "Mine either! But I've got to hand it to you and your wife, mister. You're one hell of a team!"

"Yes," Joel answered quietly. "That we are." Beneath the broad brim of the white hat, his bronzed face broke into a delighted grin. "And I can't wait to tell her so!"

The group around him murmured excitedly. Cupid clapped him on the back. "We're all pulling for you, man. You and she deserve a long vacation after what you've been through. What a story that was! I've got a little beach house at Malibu. If you'd like to use it, it's yours for the asking."

"Well, thank you. That's very generous of you." Joel

glanced over at Samantha. She was still engaged in conversation with a policeman. "But I really think," he said, "that once this is settled, we'll be very anxious to get home. And, speaking of 'settled,' I hope you'll excuse me while I go tie up a few loose ends."

Joel's long strides quickly took him to the police car in which Brad and Monroe sat. He bent to peek through the window, which was rolled down. Brad sat slumped in the seat, staring straight ahead. Monroe was crumpled in the opposite corner.

"I'm afraid I beat you out again, Brad," he said more calmly than he'd ever imagined possible.

The policeman stopped questioning Samantha and moved tentatively toward the car. Samantha followed. The other onlookers surged forward until they'd formed a ring around the small group.

Brad turned his icy blue stare on Joel. "Another trophy to add to your collection. You're a born winner, pal!"

"You could have been, too, Brad, if you'd followed your better instincts. Instead of looking for shortcuts."

"Don't go sanctimonious on me, Joel. That's always been one of your more nauseating qualities. Along with your ridiculous Boy Scout ethics."

"You're a real fool, Brad," Joel said evenly. "You had everything going for you until you deliberately chose to blow it all by breaking the law and hurting people who trusted you."

Brad chuckled. It wasn't the polite, polished laugh of a P.R. man. "You don't know what the hell you're talking about! Everything's always come up roses for you— good old dependable Joel! You've been a winner all of your life—plenty of money and security. You don't know what it is to have to scramble. Well, I do."

"I'd say slither might be more appropriate," Joel said, his tone chilling.

"Call it what makes you happy. When you offered me the job at Hyperspace, out of the goodness of your heart, for old times' sake, as it were—I jumped at it! I realized that for once in my life, I would have the chance to beat you easily. To grind your face in the dirt. Even though, as usual, you were in charge. Head of your own company by the age of thirty!" Brad looked at him with hatred.

Joel took a deep breath. "You know, Brad," he said quietly, "twenty-four hours ago I would have given almost anything to get my hands on you, but suddenly it's enough to accept that very shortly you're going to be receiving your mail at a state-run institution."

He moved away from the car and turned to look into his wife's white face. Her turquoise eyes were glimmering with unshed tears. She was feeling his pain as much as he, Joel realized. In all of their time together, he had never felt more keenly the unwavering power of their love.

"If we don't hurry," he said huskily, oblivious to the interested spectators and the hovering policeman, "we're going to miss the Thin Man reruns, on the late show."

Samantha smiled tremulously. "I've always liked Nick and Nora. They're quite a team."

"Just like us?"

"Just like us."

Joel moved forward and enveloped his wife in his arms. "I've been so worried about you," he said, his lips against her hair.

Samantha slid her hand up to caress his face. "I'm fine—now that you're here."

Joel's enthusiastic band of supporters murmured their approval at the couple's reunion. Hans Solo gave Cupid a playful shove. "Now's your chance, buddy," he encouraged.

The cherubic figure stared quizzically at the interplanetary hero, then a slow grin spread over his face. Drawing back on his bow, he shot a blunt-tipped arrow into the California night. His act inspired a wave of clapping among the onlookers, but Joel and Samantha were too engrossed in admiring the wedding ring he'd just placed on her finger to join in the applause.

— 12 —

SAMANTHA AND JOEL talked for most of the three hours and forty minutes of the flight home, oblivious to their exhausted state. They had a lot of catching up to do. They'd been separated for more than a day, and a lot had transpired during that time.

They had virtually no time alone together until they boarded the plane at dawn. First of all, they'd had to go to the police station for a debriefing session. Then a member of the police department followed them to the motel so that they could return Amanda and the Western clothing Joel had borrowed from the rodeo rider, as well as pick up their luggage. The Garfield suit was left with the sleepy, irate innkeeper, who was persuaded to take the costume back to the rental company in exchange for a generous tip. Finally, the policeman chauffeured them to the airport.

"So the dog growled and Brad came to the window?" Joel asked.

Samantha nodded vigorously. "Yes. Believe me, I had to think fast. I decided my best strategy would be to convince Brad that I was interested in a share of his action and that a side benefit of striking a deal with me would be exploring our 'mutual attraction.'"

"Pretty big gamble, wasn't it?" Joel asked carefully.

Samantha entwined her fingers with his. "Yes," she agreed. "But I had to make the most of my situation and depend on my wits to carry me through. If I'd signaled you, our chances of nailing Brad legally would have been

168

marginal at best. Fortunately, a good detective is always prepared—just like a Boy Scout."

"Hmmm . . ."

"When Brad sent me into the kitchen to pour the Scotch, I slipped a pill into his glass. The drug wasn't intended to knock him out, just make him sick as a dog. If I'd put him under, he would have awakened at some point, figured out I was on to him, and then fled, probably waiting a long time before renegotiating another deal."

"Yes," Joel agreed, "or, in the interest of expediency, he might have made another contact and moved so swiftly we wouldn't have been able to catch him."

"You're beginning to think like a detective, darling."

Joel clasped her hand more tightly. "It's very helpful when you're married to one, Sam. Now go on—"

"My next move," she continued, "was to get Brad out of the cabin—in case Miss Gable or someone else showed up. I also figured he couldn't get too amorous while he was driving. The drug I gave him requires about thirty minutes or so to take effect, and I counted on his being very uncomfortable by the time we reached Los Angeles."

"But, Sam, didn't the medication wear off eventually? You were with him for over twenty-four hours," Joel said, keeping his voice matter-of-fact.

"Nope. Because after we got to the hotel, I slipped more pills into every glass of water I gave him! I kept hoping I'd get a chance to call you, but Brad never went to sleep. He just got sicker and sicker—blamed it on a flu bug at first—and then he finally caught on . . ."

Joel squeezed her hand. "What happened?" he asked tensely.

"Well, fortunately, it was midafternoon by then and he was in a hurry. He tied me up, but decided he couldn't leave me there for the hotel maid to discover. So he took me with him, rented a costume for me, and we entered Jordan Monroe's mansion arm in arm, smiling. My smile may have been a little forced since Brad had an iron grip on my arm . . ."

"You're lucky he didn't dump you off in some deserted area," Joel said grimly. "My God, Sam! He could have, you know."

Samantha leaned closer and stroked his face lovingly. "No, darling. He likes playing it close to the edge, remember? Once he was on to me, he figured you'd show up sooner or later. He gambled on later, thinking it'd take you a long time to pick up our trail. He said he was sorry as hell he'd have to miss seeing your face when you found your wife tied up in the billiards room of Monroe's mansion, and him long gone."

Joel muttered something indistinguishable under his breath. Then the obvious struck him. *"Tied up?* How did you get loose, Sam?"

Her bright blue eyes sparkled with mischief. "Well, actually, it was plain old luck, darling."

"Oh?" he said, his voice musing.

"The billiards room is downstairs—at the back of the mansion. Brad shoved me down several hallways before he decided where to leave me. He tied me up, stuffed a handkerchief into my mouth, and disappeared to conduct his business with Monroe. I must have sat there trussed up like a mummy for fifteen minutes! And then I heard giggling and laughing outside the open window."

"Lovers," Joel murmured, beginning to understand.

"Yup. I hopped all over that damned room in my chair; I groaned, knocked into furniture . . . Someone finally heard the noise, even over the outrageous din of the party. A group of guests came in through a patio door next to the billiards room, and untied me." Samantha smiled smugly.

"But what did you tell them, darling? I mean, they must have thought the position they found you in was a bit . . . unusual. Didn't they want to call the police immediately?"

Samantha chuckled. "Most of them were already well on their way to feeling no pain, so they didn't question my story when I told them my 'date' and I had been playing kinky games, and that he'd gotten angry and left me 'to think things over.'"

Joel shook his head in disbelief. "Sam, you're something else."

"I'm glad you think so," she replied, snuggling closer to him.

"I missed you like crazy," he whispered.

"Darling, I'm so proud of the way you handled things."

He raised an eyebrow. "Accurately translated, that means you're proud of the restraint I showed." A smile touched his lips. "And at the risk of immodesty, I must say I am, too. I honestly never thought I'd see the day when I could stand by and watch my wife kissing another man."

Samantha touched his arm. "If it's any consolation, I *hated* every minute of it. But it was, I'm afraid, necessary."

"I know," Joel replied evenly. "Now—I do have another question."

"Shoot."

"Who called the police?"

Samantha reached over to trace his magnificently dimpled chin. "I did—from the suite adjoining the one where Monroe and Brad met. Boy! I must have listened outside a dozen doors before I found that unsavory duo. Anyway, the police chief happens to be an old friend of my father's and, although he was at home with the flu, he promised me the L.A.P.D.'s full cooperation."

"Friends in high places," Joel murmured. "Sam, you handled everything beautifully!" His loving gaze rested on her glowing face.

Samantha's eyes reflected the same deeply felt emotion. "Thanks, darling," she said huskily. In an excited tone, she added, "Oh, Joel! We've got him—dead to rights! The tape recorder and camera both provide admissible evidence in court if there's a credible foundation. And I, as a licensed investigator, certainly have that."

She linked her arm through his, snuggling close. "Now darling, enough about my exploits. I want you to fill me in on everything that went on with you—especially concerning that Pink Panther who kept twirling her whiskers in your direction..."

Arm in arm, Joel and Samantha entered the agency. Miss Davenport swiveled around in her desk chair. "Well, it's nice to see you two. Took your sweet time getting home, didn't you? Phone's been ringing off the hook. I've had all I can do to handle things by myself."

Joel chuckled. In a low voice he said to Samantha, "Some things never change."

"Keeps one humble," Samantha whispered back.

Watson sauntered out from his napping place behind the filing cabinet, and with his natural feline grace, leaped into Samantha's arms.

"Hi there, big boy! Have you missed us?"

For an answer, the cat purred contentedly and then his large green eyes focused on Joel, who reached out to stroke him. To everyone's surprise, Watson nuzzled the proffered hand. "Joel!" Samantha cried with delight. "Watson didn't bite you!"

Joel smiled mischievously. "They say absence makes the heart grow fonder."

Miss Davenport rose from her chair. Joel and Samantha exchanged surprised glances. The little old lady was wearing a bright blue dress, instead of her usual drab attire. A slight pink colored her cheeks. "Everything went well, I assume?" she asked gruffly.

Samantha's eyes sparkled. "Better than that. Not only did we nab our thief, but we amassed strong legal evidence against him. After the trial, he's going to be busy sorting prison laundry for a long time, I think." Smugly she added, "Joel and I made a very good team."

"That's fortunate," Miss Davenport answered crisply. "Amateurs are usually just in the way."

Joel merely arched an eyebrow. "If it hadn't been for

Samantha's guidance, I could well have screwed things up," he admitted, easing an arm around his wife's shoulders and drawing her close.

"I'm certain you did your best under the circumstances," Miss Davenport muttered, regarding him solemnly. Then, to their surprise, she stretched up on her tiptoes and delivered an unexpected kiss to his cheek.

Before either he or Samantha could register verbal shock, Miss Davenport placed her hands on her hips. "Have you two seen a newspaper?" she demanded accusingly.

Samantha allowed the golden ball of fur in her arms to leap to the floor. "No, we haven't," she answered. "We took a cab straight from the airport. As a matter of fact, we haven't even picked up my car at the train station yet."

"Then come here," Miss Davenport ordered, motioning them to join her. "I want to show you something."

They gathered around Samantha's desk where a newspaper lay open to an article circled in red. "Read this!" the secretary commanded.

Samantha and Joel, their arms around each other's waists, scanned the headline in the morning edition of *The Daily Journal:* "Midwestern Private Investigator Zaps Video Game Thief in California."

As they finished reading the article, Samantha looked incredulously from Joel to Miss Davenport. "The police chief told me he was going to do something for me—in memory of my father. He must have had a hand in this."

"The important thing is," Miss Davenport said with more enthusiasm than Samantha had heard her express in a long time, "that ever since the morning edition came out, our phone's been ringing constantly. I've made notes on all of the calls. You can return them later, Samantha." The old lady's face actually glowed as she added, "It's going to be just like it used to be. We're going to have more business than we can handle!"

"I can't believe it—this is wonderful!" Samantha exclaimed. "I'll bet the same thing's happening at Hyperspace, too, because Joel's firm is mentioned in the article. We couldn't have bought better advertising!" She hugged Joel. "Partner, I believe things have taken a turn for the better."

"We weren't really doing so badly before, Sam, but you're right. In this particular instance, the criminal actually lent us a helping hand." A thoughtful look passed over Joel's face before he said firmly, "Now, Miss Davenport, if I could prevail upon you to type a contract for me, I'd be grateful."

"What are you talking about, Joel?" Samantha asked, genuinely puzzled.

"Shhh, darling. I know now how *exacting* detective work is, so I want to make sure everything's down in writing—for the files."

To Samantha's complete amazement, Miss Davenport seated herself docilely at her desk, inserted paper in the ancient Underwood, and waited for Joel to begin dictating.

"This document should read like any other important, official record," he said. "I'll leave the legalese up to you, Miss Davenport, but here's the gist of what I want to say." He turned Samantha to him, his hands on her slender shoulders. "Joel Loring acknowledges Samantha Lacey Loring's resourcefulness and competency, her ability to work well with a trainee. Furthermore, he makes formal apology for having been unable to grasp the depth of his wife's dedication and professionalism, until he actually became her partner in solving a crime. It's true he always supported her in her occupational choice, but looking back, he realizes he didn't view her intention to restore this agency to full-line investigation as sufficiently important. For that, he is truly sorry and—"

"Darling," Samantha interrupted, "this is sweet of you, but—"

"Don't jump in yet, Sam, love. I'm not finished," Joel admonished gently. He moved his hands to the sides of her face, allowing his fingers to trace the lovely curve of her cheekbones. Miss Davenport turned expectantly in her chair, her fingers still poised primly over the keys.

"I want an—" Joel paused for a moment, trying to think of the word he needed. "Addendum," he concluded. He looked into Samantha's eyes, mesmerized by the turquoise glimmer from the sunlight streaming in the window. That same radiance kissed the tumbled blond curls, turning them to gold. She was so precious to him. If anything had happened to her . . . He couldn't imagine a life without the joys of Samantha's ubiquitous charm, clever wit, or the dependable strength that was as much a part of her as her irrepressible spirit.

"I love you, Sam—the whole woman—right down to your gumshoes," Joel said softly, the thrust of his emotion so strong he was barely aware of Miss Davenport's rhythmic typing in the background.

Miss Davenport's clacking keys surged to a crescendo and then, with a flourish, she hit the period and came to an abrupt stop. "Now, Joel, you must sign this," she insisted. "That is, if you want this to be official."

"Oh, I do, I do," Joel responded. Reluctantly, Samantha stepped out of the circle of his arms, allowing him to sign the document.

When he'd finished, Miss Davenport bestowed a beaming smile on the couple. "I'd like to say something for the record, too," she said. "Joel, when you first insisted on working with Samantha on your own case, I didn't approve. But one privilege of being older is that you're allowed to change your mind." She crossed her arms, as if daring anyone to disagree with her. When neither Samantha nor Joel said a word, Miss Davenport continued. "I think, as it turns out, you two probably learned a lot from working together. Perhaps your commitment to each other has even been strengthened. At any rate, no one should live without love, as I have. I simply want to say that I admired your mother's and father's marriage—although their relationship was not an easy one. Detectives don't live in rose-covered cottages. More often they live on the streets, or in seedy hotels. However, Samantha, your father's job was an essential part of him. Your mother understood that. I think Joel does, too—now. Anyway, your mother and father had a marvelous relationship. They supported each other in the best and worst of times, and I . . ."

"Yes?" Samantha prompted, eager to encourage her testy secretary in her unusual display of emotion.

Miss Davenport cleared her throat. "I admire your marriage just as much."

Samantha was genuinely touched. She hugged the frail woman as tears burned against her eyelids. Stepping away, she said tenderly, "Thank you for telling us this."

"I appreciate your compliment, too," Joel added sincerely, slipping his arm around his wife's waist.

"You're welcome, I'm sure," Miss Davenport returned haughtily, but in a softer tone than usual. "Now why don't we have coffee?"

Samantha and Joel exchanged glances. Both were eager to go home, to be alone together, but neither was willing to ignore Miss Davenport's kind overture. Something special had just passed among the three of them. The secretary's emotions ran as deeply as did most people's, but she guarded those emotions carefully. People had to prove themselves to the cynical old woman before she graced them with her approval. Perhaps she'd been afraid Joel would never understand his wife's unorthodox profession, that Samantha would give up her job for her marriage. Or maybe she feared Joel was merely a handsome face without substance. Whatever, Samantha knew they'd put the old lady's fears to rest.

"Let's postpone having that cup of coffee for a little while, Miss Davenport," Joel said, his thoughts seemingly in perfect harmony with Samantha's. "I have a little gift I want to present to my wife—and I'd like you to be in on the presentation."

Miss Davenport squared her thin, narrow shoulders

and answered solemnly, "I'd be honored." Turning to Watson, who was sniffing around Samantha's desk drawer where the catnip was kept, she said, "Wouldn't we?" The cat padded lazily over to the trio and assumed his haunches-down-paws-crossed position for the ceremony.

A tantalizing half-smile crossed Joel's face. "This seems to be the best time to give you this particular item, Sam. I've carried it around for a while, waiting for the perfect moment," he added mysteriously. Reaching deep into his pocket, Joel produced a tiny velvet box. "With my love, darling," he said tenderly, placing the container in her hands.

Gingerly, she opened the gift. Inside, nestled in a silken bed, lay a chain of seed pearls with a tiny gold magnifying glass attached. Samantha carefully lifted the necklace and its dainty, symbolic charm to the light. "Oh, Joel, it's the most thoughtful, most lovely—" For once in her life, words failed Samantha. Silently, she slipped into her husband's embrace.

"I'm glad you like it, Sam," Joel murmured huskily. Then, conscious of Miss Davenport, he said lightly, "I think it's more 'you' than the Sherlock Holmes hat. But equally representative of who you are and what you're about, darling."

"It's absolutely perfect," Samantha breathed. "I'll always treasure it. Isn't it wonderful, Miss Davenport?"

The secretary examined the jewelry. Squinting through her spectacles, she announced, "Yes, indeed! And I believe it's the real thing, too, Samantha. You'll have to take good care of this. Doesn't pay to be careless, you know."

Samantha suppressed a chuckle. "You're absolutely right, Miss Davenport," she answered respectfully.

The telephone jangled. With a gleam in her eye, Miss Davenport hurried across the room to answer it. "Lacey—no, I mean—Loring Detective Agency, full-line investigation. May I help you?"

Joel shot Samantha a triumphant smile. "Looks as if

I've finally been accepted for the all-around good fellow that I am."

Samantha gave him an exaggerated wink. "Yes, darling, I believe you've finally managed to pass muster!"

Joel lifted the necklace to Samantha's neck and fastened the clasp, as Miss Davenport took down notes from the caller. "You know, Sam, I think now that things are getting back to normal—correction, better than normal—we should sneak out of here and go home. What do you say?"

Samantha looked into his handsome face. Joel smiled suggestively. She'd proved a lot of things to herself over the last few days, had even surprised herself on occasion with her ability to improvise quickly, to meet difficult challenges. But one thing she'd never be able to conquer was the overwhelming effect of her husband's smile. Not that she wanted to.

"I say, darling, there's nothing in the world I'd rather do right now, but perhaps we ought to wait until Miss Davenport's off the phone—see if she can get along without me for the rest of the day."

The old secretary's hearing was obviously still quite sharp. She covered the mouthpiece with her hand. In a loud whisper she said firmly, "You two run on home. I'm certain you have lots of things to attend to. The last time I saw your philodendron, it looked as if it needed watering. No telling what condition it's in by now."

Samantha and Joel stood staring in amazement at Miss Davenport. The old lady started to turn her attention back to the telephone conversation, but when she noticed the couple still lingering in the office, she made a scooting motion with her hand. "Go on!" she whispered fiercely.

"I think, darling," Samantha said eagerly, "that Miss Davenport means business."

"No doubt about it," Joel agreed, taking her hand and pulling her toward the door.

"My!" Samantha exclaimed. "You *are* in a rush, darling! Are you that worried about your prize philoden-dron?" Playfully, she leaned her head on his shoulder.

"Yeah," Joel murmured huskily, his mouth sliding toward hers. "I simply can't wait to get my hands on a watering can—among other things."

WONDERFUL ROMANCE NEWS!

Do you know about the exciting SECOND CHANCE AT LOVE/TO HAVE AND TO HOLD newsletter? Are you on our *free* mailing list? If reading all about your favorite authors, getting sneak previews of their latest releases, and being filled in on all the latest happenings and events in the romance world sounds good to you, then you'll love our SECOND CHANCE AT LOVE and TO HAVE AND TO HOLD Romance News.

If you'd like to be added to our mailing list, just fill out the coupon below and send it in…and we'll send you your *free* newsletter every three months — hot off the press.

☐ *Yes, I would like to receive your free SECOND CHANCE AT LOVE/TO HAVE AND TO HOLD newsletter.*

Name _____

Address _____

City _____ **State/Zip** _____

Please return this coupon to:

    Berkley Publishing
    200 Madison Avenue, New York, New York 10016
    Att: Irene Majuk

Second Chance at Love®

All of the above titles are $1.95
Prices may be slightly higher in Canada.

Available at your local bookstore or return this form to:

SECOND CHANCE AT LOVE
Book Mailing Service
P.O. Box 690, Rockville Centre, NY 11571

Please send me the titles checked above. I enclose _____ Include 75¢ for postage and handling if one book is ordered; 25¢ per book for two or more not to exceed $1.75. California, Illinois, New York and Tennessee residents please add sales tax.

NAME _____

ADDRESS _____

CITY _____ STATE/ZIP _____

(allow six weeks for delivery)   **SK-41b**